THE GREAT DEER

CONNOR WHITELEY

No part of this book may be reproduced in any form or by any electronic or mechanical means. Including information storage, and retrieval systems, without written permission from the author except for the use of brief quotations in a book review.

This book is NOT legal, professional, medical, financial or any type of official advice.

Any questions about the book, rights licensing, or to contact the author, please email connorwhiteley@connorwhiteley.net

Copyright © 2023 CONNOR WHITELEY

All rights reserved.

DEDICATION

Thank you to all my readers without you I couldn't do what I love.

CHAPTER 1

Professor Aleshia O'Kin had always loved history with a rather extreme passion. She loved running all over the Realm from the snowy and rainforest covered Northern regions all the way down to the desert central regions, and even down further to the strange south of the Realm.

If there was history to find, discover and explore Aleshia would be there hoping to learn everything about that little slice of history. It was amazing and Aleshia really loved her job.

Especially as if it meant she got to work each day next to her stunning sexy husband Charlian.

But as Aleshia stood in the dark corridor of the National Realm Museum, she hated to think that Charlian wasn't there with her. He was busy getting some of the last supplies for their expedition to the far south, and normally Aleshia would never have gone with him.

There was just something so amazing and

peaceful for Aleshia as a historian in the Museum. The Museum for her was a place of knowledge, peace and there were so many lessons to learn here, that non-history people always missed.

Aleshia flat out loved coming here as a teenager and young adult when she went to university, she used to spend hours here studying and reading and looking at each of the historical finds and hoping that would solve her own problems.

And amazingly enough they did. Once Aleshia had had an awful breakup with a boyfriend and he had abused her verbally, physically and spread tons of foul rumours about her. So Aleshia came to the museum and relooked at the history of a Queen of an ancient empire. The same had happened to the Queen, but survived. That same Queen had actually survived a lot, so Aleshia knew, just knew that things could get better, and she did not need to drop out of university.

Aleshia was so glad she didn't. Otherwise she never would have been one of the top independent historians in the entire Realm.

After her and her husband's last expedition to investigate the history of the Ingnic Empire, they had been made famous. Extremely famous. Every institution, magazine and anything with even the slightest interest in history had hounded them both for exclusive articles.

Sure Aleshia and Charlian had made tons of money, but Aleshia still wasn't sure if she liked it. She loved history, the exploration and the studying. But now she was so famous, she didn't really know if working in history was still her love.

The wonderful smell of mustard, lavender and lemons made Aleshia smile as she knew that the corridor she was standing in was perfectly clear, and that excited Aleshia. It meant that whatever she wanted to look at would be clear, and her view wouldn't be obscured by any dirty fingerprints and whatever else people spread on the glass cabinets.

All too well from her university days, Aleshia knew exactly what disgusting things people spread on glass cabinets.

But today Aleshia just wanted to see the Museum here in the Capital. Or more specifically as she had told her husband multiple times, she wanted to see one single thing in the museum.

Aleshia had always, always had a soft spot for the South of the Realm, it was covered in lush rainforests, deserts and mountains. But she loved how over a thousand years ago the South was covered in tribes and there was one tribe that she truly loved to study.

The Rouble Tribe was a short lived tribe in the far, far South of the Realm who lived in the rainforest on the modern day border of the Realm. They were famous for their creative mythology, art of war and they were home to some of the finest artists in the ancient world.

Aleshia wasn't keen on the fact the tribe only survived two hundred years, but she was amazed how the tribe had managed to create mythologies, pantheon of Gods, Goddesses and Demi-gods that rivalled some of the older and longer living empires.

The Rouble were creative people and that was why Aleshia loved studying them. She once described the tribe as whatever another culture could create in ten years, the Rouble would create it in a month.

And Aleshia still believed that wholeheartedly. From all her studies of history, cultures tended to create their religions and mythologies and folklore over hundreds (if not thousands) of years.

But by the end of their first year, the Rouble tribe had created those three things, and in all honesty their mythology was more creative and larger than most of the largest Empires Aleshia had studied.

The sound of people walking, talking and laughing filled the air as the Museum opened properly and Aleshia realised she had to focus on why she was actually here.

In front of her in the dark Museum corridor was the sole surviving Deer statue of the Rouble Tribe. It wasn't just any old deer (that never would have interested Aleshia).

Instead it was a large white deer made from clay and it was half-man and a half-deer. The horns were long, twisted and fragile and Aleshia was rather impressed the deer statue looked so good after a thousand years.

This was what Aleshia hoped to research on her expedition. Aleshia wanted to find out what the Great

Deer was in Rouble culture, in all their writings, drawings and art the Great Deer was depicted but no one ever explained fully what it meant.

There were plenty of theories floating around but Aleshia wasn't sure if any of them were evidence-based, or simply made up by historians for fun.

Aleshia felt pulses of excitement run up her spine as she realised that soon she would have her answers. She couldn't believe she was finally getting to go to the rainforest, and Aleshia was finally going to research one of her favourite tribes.

Aleshia gave the deer statue a final look and let the excitement build up, before she walked away to find her husband and return to the expedition.

She really wanted to get back and start the hunt for the truth.

Aleshia was more excited than she thought humanly possible.

CHAPTER 2

Professor Charlian O'Kin was really enjoying his new promotion from Honourary Professor to real professor after him and his sexy wife Aleshia rewrote the history books on the Ingnic Empire.

At first Charlian had been beyond thrilled at all the amazing attention, money and fame it had bought them both, but then the different conferences and opportunities had led them away from each other. Charlian flat out hated that.

Charlian had stopped agreeing to do talks about how he had rewritten the history books with a series of great finds. He just wanted to be with his wife and return to what they both loved doing, that was exploring, learning and studying historical cultures.

And finally they were getting to do that again.

Charlian stroked his dragon Octon's large fiery orange scales as they both stood in the middle of a large cobblestone square and the Museum crew finished loading her up with all the supplies he had ordered.

The square was beautiful as it was surrounded by

wonderful little stone buildings and shops and even a couple of musicians were singing in the square. Charlian had no idea why, considering he was the only person besides the crew around.

The air was wonderfully crisp and smelt amazing with its hints of lavender, jasmine and fresh tea that probably meant someone had left a window open in one of the Museum's Tea rooms where only the privileged and right and proper people went to.

Charlian was more than glad he had never been. He had been invited more times than not, but those rooms and all those elitist people were political and awful that it was just wasn't worth the bother.

And it would be a bother to Charlian.

The crew were clearly working hard but every so often Charlian made to frown at them to make the crew continue working. Judging by their looks, smiles and even some flashing aimed at Charlian, he realised that these people clearly imagined him as some historical god that had all the power in the history world.

But Charlian wasn't sure he wanted it.

When him and Aleshia first got together they had spoken about their goals, dreams and aims. Both of them had wanted to be powerful and influential in the history community, but now they were Charlian wasn't sure if he wanted any of it.

He had only ever wanted Aleshia.

Charlian felt Octon move as he stroked her scales making him focus on what was happening. The museum crew were all done loading Octon up and now all Charlian needed was Aleshia to return from her little trip.

Of course she would be late, Charlian really hoped she wasn't too late. He had never been to this particular part of the rainforest before, so he didn't know what to expect.

All he knew for sure was that the expedition crew, camp and the two of them needed to be completely set up by nightfall because that was when all the monsters, animals and creatures came out.

Thankfully Charlian still had enough military contacts left over from his own military days to get them two weapons and some rainforest defences. Aleshia had laughed at him at first about the need for defences.

She wasn't laughing a few seconds later.

Charlian had served in the rainforests of the Realm from time to time in the military and he had lost tens of friends to the massive snakes, monstrous boars and even the various supernatural creatures that stalked the rainforest at night.

The defences were needed, and as long as they didn't stay out after nightfall they wouldn't be in too much danger. But Charlian still hated everything about this expedition except from the chance to spend time with his beautiful wife.

"Come on tha boss," Octon said, "what ya thinking 'bout the trip?"

Charlian just looked at Octon. She had been with

him on every trip into the rainforests with the military, she knew the answer to that question.

"Come on boss, we ain't gonna fight orks or goblins again,"

Charlian nodded slightly. She wasn't wrong about that, but everything still made Charlian nervous. Aleshia had never been to somewhere this dangerous before, Charlian just wanted, needed to protect her.

"Hello sexy," Aleshia said quietly kissing her husband.

Charlian hadn't even noticed she was walking towards him. He kissed back. Hard. Then he helped her up on Octon.

He was about to get on himself when he just stared at Aleshia, admiring her smooth beautiful face, long brown hair that he loved to run his fingers through and her seductive smile that would make him do almost anything.

He really, really loved her. He had to protect her no matter the cost.

He was just scared he might have to.

CHAPTER 3

When Aleshia slid off Octon and landed on the soft rainforest ground, she could not believe how hot and humid it was. She didn't even focus on all of the massive plants around her.

All she could focus on was the extreme heat.

Aleshia wondered how the hell had Charlian even managed to survive in such an awful place. It probably wasn't that extreme the heat, but to her it was. Considering she grew up in the much cooler north, this was just awful.

In actual fact, Aleshia would have much, much rather done another expedition in the truly extreme heat of the desert. At least she could easily hide in the shade if things could be too much, that was far from an option here.

Aleshia wanted to take a few steps forward towards the expedition base camp, but it was just too hot. Even Aleshia's loose-fitting tan shirt, trousers and hiking boots were just sticking to her.

In all her life Aleshia had never felt so disgusting, she didn't even want to think about all the sweat that was starting to pour off her. It was so disgusting that Aleshia was tempted just to leave and never return.

She could never let Charlian see her like this. It was bad enough he was behind her talking to Octon.

Then Aleshia forced herself to focus on the mission at hand. She was a professor of Pre-Realm history and she had to find out what the White Deer meant to the Rouble tribe. That was why she was here, that was what she had to focus on.

Aleshia tried to take a few steps but the heat and the humidity and the sweat on her just drained her energy. It felt like she had been running in a desert and then thrown into a cold lake of water.

Rainforests were so weird.

Aleshia focused on how loud the rainforest was. She never expected to hear so many noises from the shrieking of different animals in the distance being attacked to the humming of other wildlife to the screaming of massive animals.

The entire rainforest didn't even sound musical in the slightest, it all sounded like each noise was at all-out war with each other.

Aleshia just covered her ears and hoped she would learn to tune out the noise after a while.

But the smell had to be the worst thing about the rainforest. There must have been some plant nearby that Aleshia hated, because all she could smell was rotting flesh.

Aleshia had done some research before she commissioned the expedition and she had heard plenty about the wildlife in this part of the world. Including some of the deadliest, stinkiest and colourful plants in the entire Realm.

It was all contained here and right now, Aleshia hated the smell of rotting flesh. She was pretty sure the smell was that strong it was going to get into her clothes and ruin them. Aleshia had sadly had that experience too many times before.

And she had only just bought this new outfit. Damn it!

Aleshia almost jumped as Charlian wrapped his arms around her. Then they both realised how sweaty and disgusting they were, but they didn't pull away, they simply pressed their bodies against each other.

After being with Charlian for decades, Aleshia just excepted they were perfect for each other and they was nothing they weren't comfortable with each other saying or doing.

But after a few moments, the feeling of their sweaty bodies was a bit much so Aleshia pushed away and forced herself to walk towards the base camp.

As Aleshia walked through the amazing dense rainforest, she was amazed at the size of some of these trees. Most of them were massive thick brown trees that raised maybe a kilometre into the sky, but some were probably tens of kilometres tall.

It made no sense to Aleshia, but then she wasn't a geologist or ecologist, she focused on the history. Not the environment they occurred in, although sometimes she had to double check with an ecologist to make sure her assumptions were right.

After a few minutes of travelling through the rainforest, Aleshia was shocked at how slowly they were moving. This part of the rainforest had no roads, no pathways, no nothing to help them.

So Aleshia, Octon and Charlian had to slowly crawl, climb and jump over roots and trees so they could get to the base camp. Aleshia was surprised that Octon had wanted to accompany them, she imagined Octon would just fly up into the trees and camp there.

"How you finding it?" Charlian asked.

Aleshia wanted to tell him to go away. She was too hot, sticky and disgusting to talk with him, but she made sure she was polite. She knew he was trying to be nice, but she just wanted to get to base camp and activate some of those magic air conditioning units.

She wanted to be cool.

"Aleshia!" Charlian shouted.

Aleshia jumped as she carefully climbed over a fallen log.

"Ha," Charlian said. "Still getting use to the rainforest sound,"

"More like war," Aleshia said sharply. "Did you ask me something else?"

Charlian laughed slightly. Aleshia didn't know how many times he had served in the rainforests, but he had probably seen soldiers react like her far too often when they first came to places like this. Aleshia couldn't blame the soldiers.

"Yeah babe," Charlian said, "wanted to know what you wanted to do when we arrive at the base camp?"

Aleshia kept walking across the soft soil and root covered ground. That was a good question.

"I donno know. How far along is the main camp? We need it finished by tonight, so eight hours?"

Octon flapped her wings a little more. "Yea girly. Sunset always at 6 here,"

Aleshia stopped and looked at Octon. "6? It's the height of summer…"

Aleshia was about to say more but Charlian smiled and pointed up at the canopy. She smiled that made perfect sense, with all the trees and other plants growing so high it blocked out so much sunlight that even at sunset it was pitch black on the rainforest floor.

Something Aleshia had to remind everyone later.

Aleshia, Octon and Charlian started walking again.

"We start the expedition and search tomorrow morning. But today I want everyone focused on making the base camp secure,"

Trees snapped as Octon struggled to fit through them.

"Soz peeps. Gonna fly to the camp," Octon said flapping her wings and flying straight up.

Aleshia wished she could do that, at least she

wouldn't have to listen to all the shrieking, screaming and humming of the other animals.

"Ales!" Charlian shouted. He must have walked straight past Aleshia earlier.

Aleshia ran as quickly as she could over to him and Charlian pointed up into a group of dense trees.

She instantly smiled as she saw the main base high in the trees.

Aleshia had always wanted to live in trees and now she was going to.

This was going to be an amazing expedition for sure!

CHAPTER 4

Charlian loved the unique smell of the rainforest. It was such a strange wonderfully invigorating smell that really made him feel alive, the strong hints of rotting flesh were burning his lungs, but he loved the feeling.

During his military days it had helped him tons, especially during long, late night combat patrols to stop the goblins from attacking the main camp. It was great to be back here, Charlian was really excited about this expedition.

But he really did understand what Aleshia was probably going through, judging by her face she hated the smell with a passion, and Charlian had to at first. Like all brand new cadets sent to the rainforest had been gagging for days on the immense smell, but now he got used to it in seconds.

He wasn't sure if that was worrying or a good sign that he had spent so long in the rainforest.

When Charlian and Aleshia reached the main

camp, Charlian was filled with sheer happiness, relief and pleasure as he looked around at the massive camp up in the trees.

He knew that Aleshia would love this, and if she was happy, he was extremely happy. It was amazing how the engineers and expedition crew had managed to wrap wooden huts around the massively thick trees and then create wooden bridges that linked them all.

Charlian's best guess would probably say there was about twenty different huts, including the mess and kitchen area, it was damn well impressive. Even during his military days, their main camp hadn't looked so strong.

Charlian didn't want to admit it in front of anyone, but he thought he was going to come here and find collapsed buildings, trees and much worse. But with all the platforms, huts and even little wooden ring platforms that went around each massive tree looking so solid and strong. Charlian knew he wasn't in any danger.

And that made him feel tons better, Charlian didn't realise his stomach had knotted slightly but it was relaxing now he knew that Aleshia would be safer than he originally believed.

Thank the God-king.

"Professors!" someone shouted.

Charlian turned around to see a group of expedition crew members carrying the large crates that Octon had flew in walking behind them. All the crew continued to walk through the camp except for a tall man wearing tan coloured shirt and trousers.

Charlian was amazed the man wasn't sweaty in the slightest. He really hoped the crew had found some technique to stay cool. Charlian was sweating like no tomorrow.

"I am-" the man said.

Aleshia smiled. "Lordic O'Neil, Professor of Geography, Metrology and Ecology at the University of The Realm,"

Both Charlian and Lordic looked at each other as Aleshia grabbed his hand and shook it hard. Charlian had no idea his wife was so interested in those subjects, sure Charlian had known they were being supplied with some people that they don't normally take, but he hadn't given it a second thought.

Aleshia clearly had.

"Oh Professor Lordic, may I call you Lordic?" Aleshia said, "I am a massive fan. Your work on-"

"Honey," Charlian said, trying to save Lordic.

Aleshia smiled and Charlian just loved how wide and bright her eyes were. She was so damn beautiful.

After Charlian managed to tear his eyes away from Aleshia's killer smile, he focused on Lordic for a moment. Aleshia only tended to know the most influential people in the different fields of science, but Charlian had never seen, heard or met Lordic before.

But he had to admit at least a little that Lordic did have some attractive qualities to him. Lordic had long lifeful brown hair, strong jawline and Charlian would not have been surprised if he had a six-pack under his shirt.

Charlian just hoped he didn't have any competition for his wife. He doubted it, but still.

"Maybe the Professor Lordic wants his hand back," Charlian said.

Aleshia looked at Lordic's hand that was now ghostly white. She released it. "Oh. Sorry Lordic. I never normally get like that,"

Lordic smiled. "It's okay, my dear. I get that a lot. Surely you must with your celebrity status. I must admit that I… rather excited to meet you,"

Then a young woman about his age kept up behind him and kissed him on the cheek. "Sure right babe. He couldn't stop banging on about his excitement for weeks before we came out here,"

Charlian and Aleshia just smiled at that. It was still strange to be appreciated like this, but it did feel great.

"Professors," Lordic said, "this is my wife Cassandrea O'Neil, Professor of Modern History at the University of Dragon Riders,"

Charlian and Aleshia quickly looked at each other and all four of them laughed. The two universities had a legendary rivalry that stretched back hundreds of years since their foundings. It was a massive rule of both universities not to date, talk or even look at people from the rival university.

Charlian had no idea how these two had met and gotten married.

He wasn't even sure if he and Aleshia should

acknowledge her, and that was before he considered she focused on the far less interesting Modern Realm History.

"Come on peeps, it's okay," Lordic said, "She ain't going to bite or do any pranks on us. We're grown ups now,"

All four of them nodded and went in for a group hug, something that would have gotten them kicked out of both universities back in the day.

Charlian had to admit this was an interesting start to the expedition, and he knew things were only going to get more interesting.

"Professors," Cassandrea said to Charlian and Aleshia, "I gathered everyone in the mess hut if you want to speak with them,"

Aleshia took a step forward. "Let's go and let the expedition begin!"

And that really excited Charlian.

CHAPTER 5

As Aleshia walked into the Mess Hut with sexy Charlian, Lordic and Cassandrea, she was impressed with how amazing it looked. She was expecting the wooden hut that was tied to the massive trees to look dark, damp and cramp.

In reality, it looked quite the opposite. The expedition crew had managed to create a large Mess Hut that stretched on for tens of metres and since the roof was a magic blend of thatch and leaves, it was waterproof and yet it still allowed for plenty of natural light to enter.

It was amazing.

And this was what really kicked off an expedition for her, walking into the amazing Mess area with all those young (and old) bright faces staring at her, wanting to start and help her make a major discovery.

But this time round the energy was even more intense than normal, it felt like every single crew member wanted to jump up and hug Aleshia (the famous celebrity), and everyone wanted to help her do whatever was needed to find another groundbreaking discovery.

It was a bit much, but Aleshia just grabbed Charlian's hand.

As Aleshia and the other three professors went towards the head table at the back of the mess hut, Aleshia admired the stunning woodwork done on each of the immensely long tables that stretched horizontally across the hut.

When she put the order in for them, Aleshia had expected some cheap tables like she normally got, but clearly this sponsor wanted to impress her. Each table was handcrafted with creatures, runes and historical symbols carved into each table leg and table top.

Aleshia swore under her breath a few times as she knew for a fact she was going to spend some evenings looking at each symbol to test herself.

Her love of history was maddening like that sometimes. But she loved it.

When Aleshia reached the head table, she was surprised, she had specifically ordered a smaller, dull table. Since Charlian never liked the massive imposing ones, and quite frankly Aleshia hated them.

Her crew were her friends and she was no master of them.

But this sponsor had again done something rather different. The table was painted in a thin layer of gold, but to make it look more impressive and less imposing. They must have gotten a dragon to breathe fire all over it. Creating a rather wonderful blackened gold effect.

Aleshia took a seat at the central seat at the table and sat her. She hissed as coldness shot up, she was going to have to get use to that, but at least that damn shrieking, screaming and humming sound was quieter now, or she had started to tune it out.

Aleshia was about to start talking when five very young men (probably in their first year at university) bought out a glass for each of the professors and poured in a bright orange drink.

Aleshia saw Charlian smile and lick his lips. She had no idea what it was, he clearly liked it, yet she didn't want to seem rude, ungrateful or ignorant so she didn't ask what it was.

She drank it and Aleshia's mouth was filled with the most stunning combination of sweetness, sourness and fruitiness she had ever experienced. It was flat out amazing.

Aleshia needed to ask for that again.

"Babe," Charlian whispered, "that's made from that plant that stinks of rotting flesh,"

Aleshia's stomach churned a little but she kept smiling and focused on the crew.

"Thank you everyone for coming. It means a lot that you want to become part of my team," Aleshia said.

Charlian coughed.

"Sorry, our team," Aleshia said.

Everyone laughed.

"We have just bought in some supplies from the Capital," Aleshia said, "it is my understanding that the main camp must be secured by 6 pm tonight. So as soon as this meeting is finished Professor Charlian will take you all outside and you'll help him put up the defences,"

Everyone nodded excitedly. She had no idea people could get so excited about setting up some defences. Actually she had to double check what they were with Charlian later.

"Professor Aleshia," Lordic said.

Aleshia nodded.

"I hate to say it my dear, but we don't have until 6 pm. We only have until 4 pm due to a monstrous storm that will rip through the rainforest later on,"

Aleshia just frowned. Not at Lordic but at the situation, she had been leading expeditions for decades through sandstorms, rain and even an earthquake.

But never had Aleshia had to lead an expedition in a place filled with deadly creatures that required a fortified main camp, and now there was a storm coming.

They only had four hours to finish setting up. This wasn't good. Aleshia had to focus on what was important, or everyone might suffer.

"Thank you Professor Lordic," Aleshia said, she turned to face the crew. "We will talk at dinner about objectives for the expedition and how your teams will work,"

There was a rather loud groan of disappointment. Aleshia actually found that rather sweet of everyone.

"Right now," Aleshia said, "get out of here and finish up the preparation,"

Aleshia looked at Charlian who was already standing and walking away from her. They blew each other a few kisses.

As much as the situation scared Aleshia about all the creatures that could and would kill them, she knew deep down that if anyone could save her, the crew and the other professors, it would be Charlian (with Octon's help of course).

But now she was here. The danger felt so real that she wasn't sure if she was going to regret coming here in the first place.

CHAPTER 6

Charlian couldn't believe how exhausted he was!

Charlian might not have set up those magic shield generators, magic guns and other defences for a good few years, but he hadn't remembered them being that heavy. His muscles, back and neck just ached after moving all of those pieces into place.

Thankfully it hadn't taken him anywhere near as long as he feared and judging by the weather outside, Charlian was more than pleased with that.

The sound of booming thunder, lashing rain and explosive falling trees ripped through the rainforest, so much so that Aleshia had ordered no one to leave the mess hut until the storm had calmed down. Charlian wasn't going to argue.

He had been in some extreme storms in his military days, but none where this bad. Charlian could barely hear himself think, let alone listen to the talking, laughing and fearful mutterings of the crew who weren't sat too far away from the head table.

Charlian loved the amazing smell of the food being served. He was really glad Aleshia had listened to him about getting local recipes and even asking the University scribes to write down some Rouble recipes for them.

This was probably the most amazing meal Charlian had had in ages. The main meal tonight was the Rouble equivalent of soup and it had massive chunks of goat, eatable tree bark and some exotic fruits all in the creamiest sauce Charlian had ever tasted.

It was an explosion of flavour on his tongue, and he wasn't too sure about the tree bark at first, but now he realised you couldn't take it out. It gave the dish too much flavour and texture to leave out.

Charlian was going to love this expedition for the great food alone.

As Aleshia finished up her soup, Charlian just stared at her elegant movements, amazing hair and that sexy smile.

She was more beautiful in the storm than he had ever seen her, and he knew that in amongst all the chaos of the weather, she was his eye of the storm. The beautiful calm centre where he felt safe.

"Is everything secure?" Aleshia asked as she licked her soft lips. Charlian felt as if he was becoming a schoolboy again.

"Um, yeah," Charlian said, trying to force his adult brain back into gear.

"Join me in the talk," Aleshia said with a smile as

she stood up.

Charlian stood up and tapped his spoon against the table. Everyone smiled and focused on them, Charlian was starting to feel the amazing energy of excitement build up again.

"Thanks everyone for helping out. We should be safe now," Charlian said.

A female crew member stood up at the far end of the Hut. "But Professor, is this is a dangerous mission? Are we insured for danger?"

Charlian carefully looked at Aleshia. He had no idea, but he always left the business and money side of the expeditions to her.

"Of course. If anything happens the expeditions covers all of our bills," Aleshia said.

"Thank you," the woman said sitting back down.

Aleshia bowed her head slightly. "As you know we are seeking out information and sites on the Rouble Tribe from a thousand years ago,"

Excited mutters filled the Hut. Charlian forced down his excitement.

"The Tribe survived here for 200 years and created a vast mythology and that is what we are interested in," Aleshia said. "As always all historical findings are important and we are likely to discover other remains here too,"

Charlian quietly squeaked as he loved the idea of that. Not only could they learn more about the Rouble, they could learn more about the tens of other tribes that lived here over the centuries. This was going to be epic!

Charlian stood up. "And we are focusing on the tales about the Great White Deer in their mythology. We don't know much about it besides the stories about the Great Hunts, the Blood Drinking and the war of the Deer in their creation stories,"

Charlian saw Cassandrea mutter something with a devilish smile. He was not going to be impressed if she knew something about Pre-Realm history that he and Aleshia didn't.

That would be embarrassing.

"Thank you babe," Aleshia said, "you'll be split into groups of five and sent off tomorrow to find some discoveries,"

"No!" Lordic shouted.

Charlian watched as Aleshia frowned and took two long deep breaths. He wasn't going to jump in, in all their expeditions Charlian and Aleshia had never had such an interruption.

"Something wrong, Professor Lordic," Aleshia said coldly.

Lordic stood up. "Well, my dear. The problem is the storm. My predictions guess that the storm will not stop for another day. It might stop tomorrow night, but then that is unwise to travel,"

Aleshia looked at Charlian and he just nodded at her. It made perfect sense and there was no reason to send the crew out into a dangerous storm.

Charlian had forgotten how long these storms lasted, and he really didn't have the heart to tell

Aleshia that this was a short storm.

"Okay. Thank you Lordic," Aleshia said.

"Surely a Pre-Realm Historian should know that. The storms were why these tribes were some of the last to form the Realm," Cassandrea said.

Charlian couldn't believe the cheek of that. How dare she try to show up Aleshia in front of the entire crew, that was outrageous and completely out of order.

As Charlian took a few deep breaths to calm himself down, he knew they were going to have to watch her and maybe Lordic. He wasn't going to have them ruin Aleshia's expedition.

And at the end of the day, she was Expedition Leader. Not them.

Charlian stood up again. "Instead tonight get to know each other and bond friendships. When you're in the rainforest your friends are your life. Believe me,"

Charlian shrugged a little. He had been attacked way too many times by the goblins when he was last in the rainforest to not know the importance of friends. They had saved his life too many times.

And he had saved theirs.

"Tomorrow everyone," Charlian said, "we all start studying up on the Rouble tribe and their mythology. We might be able to get some clues together,"

Everyone just sort of stopped and it took Charlian a few moments to realise what was going on.

Everyone was listening for the crackling of the Magic Shields that had intensified themselves so they blocked out most of the storm. Making it safe to move around the main camp.

And for the crew that meant, it was safe to go to the social club and bar of the camp.

Aleshia grabbed his hand. "Thank you, Professor Charlian. Everyone dismissed,"

As everyone left the Mess Hut, Aleshia led Charlian outside and across the various wooden platforms.

"Where are we going?" Charlian asked.

Aleshia pulled him close. "I need some stress relief,"

Charlian was shocked as Aleshia pulled him close and she rubbed her lower body against his.

He definitely had to help his wife calm down.

That's what good husbands did, wasn't it?

CHAPTER 7

The storm might have stopped two days later but Aleshia was seriously starting to hate the rainforest.

In any normal place having millions of gallons of lashing rain, rageful thunder and slashing wind would have made a place perfectly cool and maybe even cold the morning after.

But no, not the rainforest.

As Aleshia leant against the wooden railings of a massive wooden platform high up in the trees, she couldn't believe how disgusting she felt. It was so hot, sticky and it was a million times worse than two days ago.

Aleshia just wanted to go home, have a bath and leave this troubled rainforest. But she had a job to do first, a job she really, really loved.

Aleshia focused on the stunning rainforest around, above and below her as she took a few seconds to enjoy the view. The past two days had been so chaotic with shields failing, huts being ripped apart and even some the crew getting injured.

There was going to be so much paperwork after this expedition. Aleshia hated that, but that's what husbands were for, right?

As Aleshia stared at the massive brown trees that rose up like daggers into the rainforest canopy, she couldn't help realise how small and unimportant she felt, and that was something that she loved about history.

History taught Aleshia that everyone's lives were just spilt-seconds in the history books, and it wasn't what a normal person did that mattered in terms of history. It was what an extraordinary person did that happened.

Aleshia really hoped that her history work could give her at least a passing mention in the far future history books.

A girl could dream right?

Aleshia flicked her attention back to the large silver bracelet with black jewels attached to it that was hung around her wrist as she waited to be contacted.

After having these bracelets gifted to her on her last expedition, Aleshia had learned to love these little things. It was a type of magic communication device, so all the wearer needed to do was think of her and talk into the bracelet.

Then Aleshia would hear it.

And with every expedition member having one, Aleshia was starting to get really excited about the first great discovery that someone would call in.

Aleshia smiled as she felt Charlian's soft lips press against the top of her head and he passed her a large mug of lukewarm coffee.

"Bit cold isn't it?" Aleshia said.

Charlian smiled. "Seriously babe. In the rainforest you learn quickly not to drink hot drinks. They make you sweat more, you felt more disgusting and that just kills morale,"

Aleshia nodded. She felt like she was going to learn tons on this expedition about living in general, let alone history.

"Did the teams get off alright?" Aleshia asked.

"Not as good as me last night,"

Aleshia playfully hit Charlian, but last night was great.

"Seriously though," Aleshia said.

Charlian gave her a schoolboy smile. "Yeah. I sent off the teams the morning and judging by our research we're likely to find Rouble settlements if we start traveling south,"

Aleshia could only nod at that. If the teams went too far south then they might hit the Militarised Zone by the Realm's Southern border. She didn't want to have to answer questions from the troopers there.

Those particular soldiers were already touchy enough waiting for the next wave of trolls, goblins and whatever supernatural nightmare those wastelands decided to throw at them. Aleshia would definitely rather leave them alone.

"Did you send off those O'Neil people?" Aleshia

said bitterly.

Aleshia had no problem with Lordic whatsoever. She was actually enjoying talking to him about geography, ecology and meteorology, and then applying that knowledge to how it could have impacted the history and development of the Rouble tribe.

It was really fascinating and Aleshia was certainly going to hire him again.

But his wife was plain awful. She clearly had a bone to pick with Aleshia, especially yesterday when Cassandrea had publicly tried to humiliate Aleshia twice in the space of an hour.

Aleshia had even had to use her special Expedition Leader Powers to remove Cassendrea from the head table, and by extension she no longer had an input in the running of the expedition.

Aleshia flat out didn't trust her.

"Yeah. I sent them both off together. Lordic apologised again repeatedly," Charlian said.

"Thank you," Aleshia said. "What do you know about The Great White Deer creation story?"

Charlian's face lit up. "It's…"

"One of the more interesting and creative stories in the ancient world," Aleshia said.

"Definitely. The Rouble believed that the world was once a massive boulder floating in the Divine Realm," Charlian said.

Aleshia smiled, that was probably the most normal part of the story.

"Then in the Divine Realm the gods and goddesses were out hunting Deer one day, they attacked a group and one got separated,"

"But the Divine being didn't chase after it," Aleshia said.

"Correct,"

Aleshia gently hit him for talking to her like some dumb student.

"Sorry babe. Then that separated deer ran through the Divine Realm until they found this boulder," Charlian said. "The Deer jumped up and down on the boulder for ten years until something happened,"

"The deer's legs smashed into the boulder and it screamed in agony. Then the Divine Realm decided it didn't want the boulder anymore so the Divine Realm smashed up the deer into a pulp,"

Aleshia laughed a little. "Then the pulp was spread over the boulder and it was kicked out of the Divine Realm into our reality today,"

Charlian just looked at her and she completely agreed. It was one thing to actually read these crazy stories, but it was another thing to say them aloud and try to make them seem believable.

"After that," Aleshia said, "legend says that the Deer blood became water, the bones became mountains and the flesh and skin become the ground we walk on,"

"What about the rainforest?" Charlian said with a smile.

Aleshia wanted to throw some coffee at him, but it was a good point. Considering the Rouble Tribe lived in a rainforest that didn't have any mountains, it was strange they did include it in their creation story.

Aleshia clicked her fingers. "You know what. Trees must be the Deer fur,"

Charlian shrugged. To Aleshia it made just as much sense as the rest of it.

Aleshia's wrist vibrated. She jumped.

She took a few calming breaths as she pressed her silver communication bracelet and answered the call.

"Professor O'Kin!" a young woman shouted.

"What is it?" Aleshia asked. She didn't expect calls 30 minutes after sending everyone out.

"We've found something. Something massive. Something Mysterious. It's glowing!"

Aleshia just looked at Charlian. "You better call Octon, I think we have exploring to do,"

Charlian just smiled. Aleshia smiled too.

Finally the expedition was truly beginning and that really, really thrilled her!

CHAPTER 8

Charlian had completely forgotten how much he and Octon loved rainforests. There was just something amazing about them with their sweatiness, stickiest and how they made you feel.

As much as it pained him to know that Aleshia wasn't comfortable here in the rainforest, he loved it, and it was really making him happy to know that Octon was enjoying her time here.

In fact Charlian had barely seen her too much in the past few days. She had begged Charlian to let her hunt in the rainforest and experience the wild weather like a "good" dragon should.

Charlian had no idea when Octon became a typical or "good" dragon, but she had done so much for him in rainforests back in his military days, he felt like he owned her something. So he wasn't going to say no.

As Charlian, Aleshia and Octon flew over the rainforest which looked like a massive dark green blanket below them, it was a massive relief to Charlian to see Aleshia look more normal and like she was enjoying herself. He had to admit the warm early morning air did feel great on the skin, and it definitely dried out their clothes.

In amongst the howling sound of the wind as they flew, Charlian just smiled at the little tune that Octon was humming to herself. It was such a wonderful merry, joyful and musical tune.

Then she stopped and started to hover in the air.

"What tis woman report boss?" Octon asked.

Charlian hugged Aleshia as if to prompt her to explain. "We don't know,"

Aleshia carefully turned around and climbed over Charlian to get to the supplies on Octon's back. Charlian had wanted to get the rope and other supplies for her, but Aleshia stressed how capable she was.

"We only know it's glowing," Charlian said.

Octon nodded. Aleshia screamed as she slipped. Grabbing onto the saddle before she fell.

"Don't do that," Charlian said with a smile.

Octon winked at him.

Charlian blew Octon a quick kiss. She had a terrible sense of humour, so Charlian got up and carefully walked over to the supplies and helped Aleshia back up.

She didn't look impress, so Charlian just got out the ropes and tied them to the saddle on Octon.

"Are tha ropes long enough boss?" Octon asked.

Charlian looked at Aleshia. He didn't know. He had never had to climb down into the rainforest before.

Aleshia nodded and put on her harness and made sure she was securely tied to the rope and Octon.

Charlian did the same.

After a few minutes they were both perfectly safe in their harnesses and Aleshia kissed him quickly.

"In case you don't make it," Aleshia said with a devilish smile.

"Not funny," Charlian muttered as he looked over the side of Octon.

He had never been a fan of highs and this certainly didn't help. It was easily thirty metres until they hit the rainforest canopy and then it was easily another fifty metres until they reached the rainforest floor.

This wasn't going to be easy.

Charlian felt his stomach churn, tighten and flip as he realised snakes and other creatures would be hiding in the canopy waiting for unsuspecting birds to drop through.

Charlian didn't want to die.

"Honey," Aleshia said, "you look a bit pale. You okay?"

"Why couldn't we walk through the rainforest like normal people?" Charlian asked.

Aleshia kissed him. "Because where's the fun in that?"

Aleshia slid off Octon. Charlian flew forward.

Then he saw how she was perfectly safe in her harness and carefully lowering herself towards the rainforest below.

"Right boss," Octon said, "remember to three pulls on the rope and that tells me you're done,"

Charlian nodded and slid off Octon.

He hated the feeling of nothing being under him. It felt so unnatural as Charlian started to slid down the rope and using his hands to control his speed.

Charlian wasn't a fan of the horrible rough texture of the rope. He didn't know if he could manage about fifty metres of climbing on this.

Charlian kept going. He kept climbing. He had to find out what the team had discovered.

By the time he reached the rainforest canopy, his arms were starting to ache and his hands felt shredded by the rope. He should have worn gloves that was for sure.

Charlian kept lowering himself as one of his feet touched the leaves and branches of the rainforest something wrapped round his leg.

Charlian screamed.

He looked down.

A blue snake was climbing up him.

Charlian screamed.

The snake raised its head.

It was preparing to strike.

Instincts took over.

Charlian grabbed it by the neck.

It hissed.

It bit Charlian.

He screamed.

He crushed its neck.

Charlian started to feel lightheaded.

He started to feel dizzy.

Charlian's vision was going.

Charlian couldn't fall from the rope, so he started to wrap the rope around himself. Making sure to tie knots in it every so often.

He had to make sure he was okay.

Charlian lost feeling in his fingers.

Then his arms.

Then his legs.

Charlian was paralysed.

And all he could think of was how he couldn't see his beautiful stunning wife.

Where was she?

CHAPTER 9

Aleshia couldn't understand how she had been so damn stupid. She should have listened to Charlian about his doubts about climbing down into the rainforest, that was stupid.

She never should have encouraged him to go along with her. She should have walked through that stupidly hot, humid rainforest to get to the team.

Aleshia hated herself as she stared at the paralysed body of her beautiful sexy Charlian in amongst all the massive brown trees that rose up high into the rainforest.

Charlian just looked so helpless, injured and in agony as Aleshia stared at him. Thankfully they had been climbing right above the team so they had helped Aleshia to get Charlian down.

Aleshia could still remember the hate, rage and fury in Octon's words at her for Aleshia's stupid idea. Aleshia couldn't blame Octon, they both loved Charlian, and it was her idea that had injured him.

Thankfully Aleshia and Charlian had both studied historical medicine at university, so Aleshia had a rough idea what herbs and plants and trees barks they needed to create a potion to reverse the effects of the snake venom.

Or the venom could continue to flow through Charlian's blood through his lungs and eventually into his brain. If the paralysis of his lungs didn't kill him quickly, the killing of his brain cells would.

Aleshia was not letting that happen to the man she loved.

Luckily the expedition members knew what Aleshia was talking about when she said the names of the ingredients, so they were running around the rainforest collecting the. Aleshia just hoped they didn't take too long.

She didn't know how long Charlian had left.

Aleshia went to kiss Charlian on the head but he had a loud moaning stop. It was probably the poor man trying to warn her about something, as heartbreaking as it was to hear him like this, she knew that it was dangerous to risk mixing fluids with poison victims.

There was a good chance Charlian's body was trying to sweat the venom out of him, so if she kissed him some of that poison sweat could enter her mouth and poison her too.

As much as it pained Aleshia to leave him, Aleshia stood up and went over to the female team leader who was leaning against a massive tree.

In all the chaos of Charlian, Aleshia had never got to ask the team leader why she had called her here in the first place. Aleshia was relieved that Cassandrea and Lordic were here, but she knew deep down it was only a matter of time.

"Professor," the team leader said.

"Team Leader…" Aleshia said, gesturing for her name.

"Patty," the woman said.

Aleshia smiled. "Good name,"

Patty pointed behind Aleshia towards Charlian. Aleshia took a deep breath of the damp hot air.

"He'll be fine as long as the other come back soon," Aleshia said. "Can we focus on what you found please?"

Patty hesitated for a few moments then she nodded and led Aleshia away from Charlian. Each step felt like a massive weight of rock was crushing her, Aleshia never wanted to be away from Charlian when he was injured.

But until the others came back, there was nothing she could do.

"We discovered it about five minutes before we call you," Patty said.

"You said it was massive and glowing?" Aleshia asked as she stepped over some roots.

"Look for yourself," Patty said pointing forward.

Aleshia finished stepping over the last of the tree roots and she gasped. Right in front of her was a massive… lake? Pond? Something else entirely?

All Aleshia saw was a massive lake-like thing filled with bright gold glowing liquid and there were little Deer statues inside the lake.

Some were made from bronze, others wood and even more were made from bones that were tied together with hair.

"Well," Aleshia said, trying and failing to think about what to say.

"And now you see why we called you," Patty said.

Aleshia wanted to impress Patty by telling her exactly what it was, but in all her decades of research and experience, she had never read about a golden lake with Deer statues.

Then Aleshia realised that she was only thinking like that because that stupid Cassandrea had gotten under her skin. Aleshia was amazing at her job and she didn't need to prove it to anyone.

"Professor, I don't remember any mention of a lake in the Rouble texts,"

Aleshia nodded then clicked her fingers. "What about in the art?"

Patty smiled and her eyes widened. "Of course Professor. We can't treat the Rouble like a normal culture. They didn't record important things in words. They recorded them in art,"

Aleshia was really pleased to have another history buff with her. Then she tried to remember what she had seen in the massive Rouble art collection book she had back at camp, she had committed each one to memory before the expedition started.

But she couldn't remember seeing it.

"Nothing," Aleshia said.

Patty frowned and subtly gestured towards Charlian.

Aleshia shrugged. There was actually a rather good chance Charlian knew something about a Golden Lake in the Rouble artwork. He was always much more into history's interpretation of the natural world than she was.

Aleshia needed him.

"The Deer statues," Patty said, calmly.

"Yeah, what about them?" Aleshia asked.

Patty smiled. "Remember how they are celebrated, worshipped and adored,"

Aleshia clicked her fingers and knelt down next to the golden glowing liquids. She carefully dipped a finger into it.

As soon as her finger touched the lake, she felt such energy and life and healing power fill her. Aleshia hadn't even realised her knees were sore before the lake filled them with energy and youthfulness.

Aleshia hadn't felt his young in decades, and it was because of this golden liquid.

She could feel Patty was staring at her wanting her to say something, or order her to bring Charlian over. But she was scared. What if this golden liquid only made you feel like this? What if it was actually poisonous? Or what if it reacted badly with the venom?

She couldn't lose Charlian.

Aleshia's silver bracelet vibrated and she slowly answered.

A young man seemed to be calling her. "Professor, we cannot. I repeat cannot find the tree bark from the *Invictous Foreverus* tree. The tree doesn't grow here,"

Aleshia's stomach tightened into a painful knot. She didn't know that at the time, but it made sense now. This humid climate would probably be too much, she clearly wasn't thinking as clearly as she should be.

But she needed that bark more than anything, it was what Charlian needed. Aleshia had to save him.

Aleshia shot up.

She ran over to Charlian. Throwing him over her shoulder.

Aleshia flew back to the lake.

Aleshia threw Charlian in.

As Charlian sunk into the liquid loud moans filled the air and Aleshia did everything in her power not to cry. She couldn't have him in pain.

Then Charlian sunk right down. Aleshia couldn't see him anymore.

He was gone.

CHAPTER 10

Charlian hated how cold the liquid was.

Charlian wanted to lash out, screamed and swim back up to the surface. He couldn't. He was trapped.

All Charlian could do as the golden liquid rose up around him and he felt his heavy fleshy body sink down deeper and deeper and deeper into the lake was… nothing.

The freezing cold golden liquid covered his eyes and every millimetre of his body as he sunk. Charlian tried to breathe but even that was becoming harder and harder.

Charlian wanted, needed to kick and scream and live. But his body was simply too paralysed.

His lungs started burning as they were starved of oxygen and Charlian knew, just knew that he was going to die.

He was never going to blame Aleshia, that sexy hot woman who had loved him so much. She had tried to save him, but it clearly wasn't working to him.

As bright white lights filled his vision Charlian wanted to laugh or smile, but his face was frozen. His lungs were burning and Charlian was in utter agony.

His vision blackened.

Then something happened.

Charlian screamed as he felt pure magical energy shoot into his body. His blood, veins and bones felt like they were being ripped open and pumped full of energy.

Charlian started to feel younger, stronger and more attractive than he had felt in decades. He started to move his fingers.

Then his arms.

Then his legs.

Then his body.

Slowly Charlian forced himself to swim back up to the top of the lake, and he exploded through the surface. Never feeling as good as he did now.

The hot sticky air of the horrible rainforest covered Charlian instantly, making his skin and clothing feel awfully sweaty and sticky. Not what he wanted, but considering he had just almost died, he really didn't care.

He was alive and that was what mattered.

Charlian wiped his eyes and saw the most beautiful woman alive looking, smiling and crying at him. Aleshia was kneeling on the ground staring at him. Charlian wasn't surprised in the slightest about how amazing it felt to see her again.

He started to swim over to her as quickly as he

could and Charlian jumped out of the lake and hugged Aleshia tight. Savouring her sexy, wonderful perfume and her smooth skin.

Charlian almost didn't want to let her go but Aleshia pulled away slightly and someone coughed behind them.

"Professor Charlian. Good to have you back," Patty said.

Charlian smiled. It really was great to be back, even in the middle of a humid rainforest surrounded by hundreds of thousands of massive brown trees and millions of creatures that would kill him at any moment.

He was glad to be back, back on the hunt for knowledge.

"I'm sorry," Aleshia said.

Charlian simply stopped her talking by tenderly kissing her once, then twice, then a third time.

"It's okay," Charlian said.

Aleshia smiled weakly at that, and Charlian pointed her and Patty back to the lake.

"Is this Rouble?" he asked.

"I have no clue Professor," Patty said, "we were wondering if you saw something like this in the Rouble Artwork,"

Charlian wasn't sure. He knew he focused a lot more on the Rouble's interpretation of the natural world compared to Aleshia, but it looked so wonderous that he was sure he would have remembered seeing it.

In the Rouble artwork, there was tons of paintings or drawings of cattle, snakes and plants. Charlian still wasn't sure where the cattle came from but that drawings were towards the end of their tribe. So maybe they bought the cattle off another tribe?

But lakes were always rare in rainforests, particularly in this area so close to the Southern border, so Charlian doubted this was natural.

"Nope," Charlian said, "never seen it before. What if this wasn't natural? But magical?"

Aleshia looked doubtful, and Charlian couldn't particularly blame her for doubting him. Either one of them focused too much on magical lore, yet considering how mixed history, cultures and magic was, they had both picked up a few pieces of knowledge along the way.

But to think magic could create a lake in the middle of a rainforest, it just seemed so doubtful.

"Oh God-King," Aleshia said.

Charlian and Patty looked at her. Charlian rarely heard her use the King's name in vain.

"What's wrong?" Charlian asked.

"What colour snake attacked you?" Aleshia asked.

"Blue,"

"And that snake didn't kill you, right?"

Charlian pretended to touch himself up in Aleshia's direction. "Nope, think I'm alive,"

"Judging by your trousers you are," Patty said.

Charlian crossed his legs quickly. "Your point?"

"My point is how big was the snake that attacked you?"

Charlian went to open his mouth then he realised what Aleshia was getting at. Snakes that normally paralysed people were larger snakes that were big enough to dislocate their jaw and eat a man whole.

The snake that attacked Charlian was far from big. It was a rather thin snake now Charlian was actually thinking about it.

Something wasn't natural about that snake.

"The size was off," Charlian said.

Aleshia clicked her fingers. "Exactly. I don't believe that snake was natural. The Rouble Tribe only ever mentioned large snakes. They rarely, rarely encountered venomous snakes that could injure people,"

Charlian nodded at that. Even though snakes these days were more than capable of paralysing people for long periods of time, the fossil record and science showed that that change in paralysis only occurred after the Rouble Tribe died off.

Meaning only one thing. That really, really annoyed Charlian.

"So this lake isn't Rouble in the slightest," he said.

Patty huffed. "Sorry Professors,"

"It's okay," Aleshia said, giving Patty a comforting hug. "But the snake that attacked Charlian wasn't from around here, and there are been no historical or modern reference to that sort of snake being here,"

Charlian nodded. "So it is far more likely this lake is magical, considering the healing powers, and that snake is sort of magical defence,"

"And the Rouble didn't use magic, did they?" Patty asked.

Aleshia and Charlian just shook their heads.

"I wonder does Professor Cassandrea know differently," Patty muttered to herself.

Charlian just watched the shock, rage and annoyance in Aleshia's eyes grow.

And he didn't blame her in the slightest.

Cassandrea was now becoming a problem.

CHAPTER 11

Aleshia couldn't believe that stupid Professor Cassandrea was actually interfering with her expedition. Aleshia had conducted, led and ran tens of expeditions and all of them had made a meaningful impact in history.

Aleshia was even famous and one of the leading experts in the history world after her last expedition. And what had that stupid woman done?

Nothing!

Aleshia just wanted to scream, shout and firmly tell that woman that she was in charge, and under no circumstances was that ever going to change.

As Octon flew over the rainforest that looked like a massive thick green blanket underneath them, Aleshia loved the feeling of Charlian's strong arms around her as they flew towards their next destination.

Apparently the stupid woman and wonderful Professor Lordic had discovered something that they knew was critical to the survival of the Rouble Tribe, but because of Aleshia's control-freak tendencies, they wished her to check it out.

Aleshia just wanted to swear at her when Cassandrea called in on the silver bracelets. But more than anything else, Aleshia just wanted the chance to prove that stupid, know it all Cassandrea wrong, and show her expedition that she knew her stuff.

It still hurt that Patty even considered Cassandrea might be able to prove Aleshia wrong. Aleshia was never delusional and she knew she didn't know everything about history, but she was sure on this.

That lake had nothing to do with the Rouble Tribe.

And before she and Charlian left, Aleshia had examined those Deer statues in the lake. It turned out they weren't Deer as such, it was a historical ancestor of the modern day Horse that historians called "The Black Horse Deer". Because of its similarities.

"Good to have ya back boss," Octon said as she slowed down over a large clearing.

Aleshia found it was a bit odd there was a clearing in the middle of the rainforest, but as Octon got closer she started to notice there were some ruins down there.

They were far too high up to see or for Aleshia to make out anything, but she was sure about the ruins.

"Can you take us down?" Aleshia asked Octon.

"Are ya gonna try to kill ma friend again?"

Aleshia frowned. She felt bad enough about the snake incident without Octon adding to it.

"I promise I won't,"

Octon made a strange groaning and moaning sound. Then she slowly started to descend into the clearing.

As soon as they entered the rainforest again, Aleshia was hit by the immense humidity of it all. Her tan coloured shirt, trousers and hiking boots were instantly covered in sweat, and that awful feeling of disgustingness came over her.

When Octon landed, Aleshia slid off and gave Octon a kiss on the snout that seemed to make the dragon blush a little. Then Aleshia walked off and was just stunned by the beauty of this clearing.

All the massive brown trees were covered in colourful flowers that made the air smell sickly sweet. It was like breathing in candy floss and caramel. The more Aleshia breathed it in, the stronger the smell grew.

It was almost too much for her to handle.

Then as the flowers caught the sunlight, Aleshia noticed something coming out of the massive colourful flowers. There were large particles of something flowing out of them.

Aleshia covered her mouth and nose and gestured Charlian to do the same. There was a small chance that those particles were drugs of some sort, so she wanted everyone to be careful.

As beautiful as the stunning flowers were,

Aleshia forced her attention away and onto the strange ruins in the clearings. They certainly weren't your normal ruins because all they were, were just the remains of wooden huts, thatch roofs and some pottery embedded in the ground.

Aleshia would have expected something far greater judging by Cassandrea's arrogant call.

The sound of drunken laughter filled the air and Aleshia started to walk towards the far end of the clearing.

And to her utter surprise, she saw Lordic, Cassandrea and the rest of their team completely naked on the ground rolling around. They weren't having "fun time", but they were just laughing on the floor.

All their clothes had been ripped off in a hurry judging by the state of them.

"What the fuck?" Charlian asked.

Aleshia just smiled. She had no idea what could make such a strong, clearly arrogant woman turn into this, and Aleshia was surprised at Lordic for going along with this too.

Unless she had been right in the first time, what if they were under the influence of drugs?

Aleshia clicked her fingers. "The Rouble worshipping ceremonies,"

"Of course," Charlian said. "They turned to drugs didn't they to connect with the Gods and Goddesses and Deer better,"

Aleshia nodded. They might not have found the

ruins of a thriving settlement belonging to the Rouble Tribe. But they might have just found out what plant they used to conduct their ceremonies.

Aleshia felt the excitement build inside her, because this was actually a major breakthrough. No historian had ever come close to working out what plants Tribes in the rainforest had used as drugs, because none of the normal drug plants grew in these conditions.

"Those flowers did look a bit dodgy," Charlian said.

Aleshia nodded then turned to Octon. "Can you return to the sky please? I don't want to risk having a dragon high on this,"

Octon rolled her eyes and looked at Charlian. He gestured back up to the sky.

"You know she likes you really," Charlian said.

"I know. I love her too," Aleshia said. "But I'm more concerned about this lot,"

Both Aleshia and Charlian just focused on the naked people rolling around on the ground laughing and now they had started to move on to kissing each other.

"We really need to stop this," Charlian said, as he went over to them.

Aleshia gently grabbed his shoulder. "You know the Rouble texts always said the users remembered what they did during the high,"

Charlian playfully hit her.

"So we could," Aleshia said, "just leave them and

teach Cassandrea a lesson,"

Charlian looked as if he was going to say no, but then he nodded.

"Fine," he said, "but the second we start to feel High. We leave,"

Aleshia nodded, that went without saying.

But as they turned to face the thatch roofs, wooden huts and pottery embedded in the ground, there was two burning questions that Aleshia had to answer.

What had once been here?

And how were they going to get Lordic, Cassandrea and their team out with them being unable to help themselves?

CHAPTER 12

Charlian was relieved not to have breathed in that horrible pollutant that those flowers were releasing into the air. The flowers looked stunning with all their bright colours, but they were clearly dangerous.

As Charlian stared at the disgusting sight of Lordic, Cassandrea and the rest of their team rolling around naked kissing each other, he had to force himself not to vomit. It was awful to look at.

The sound of their laughter was deafening and the entire situation wasn't natural, so Charlian went over to Aleshia who was standing in the middle of the clearing as she stared at the thatch roofs, wreckage of wooden huts and pottery that were embedded into the rainforest's ground.

After a little while Charlian managed to block out the sound of the drugged up laughter, and Charlian looked at Aleshia quickly.

But he had to admit she looked amazing in her

tan-coloured shirt, trousers and hiking boots. What really, really caught his eye was how Aleshia's bit of cloth that protected her mouth and nose from the pollutant made her look even more attractive than normal.

Maybe he would have to ask her to bring the cloth and wear it tonight in bed.

"What was this place?" Aleshia said, frustrated.

Charlian knelt down on the ground and carefully picked at a shard of pottery that was at his feet. He picked at it for a few seconds before he managed to pull it free.

Aleshia came over and Charlian was filled with excitement as he held a piece of history in his hand. The shard of pottery was clearly about a thousand years old, which would put it at the end of the Rouble Tribe's era. Charlian wasn't too sure if that was a good or bad thing. It meant that it possibly belong to them, but it was far from concrete proof.

Aleshia knelt down and managed to dig out a clay drinking bowl. It was beautiful with tiny threads of gold, jade and maybe even a little touch of silver in the very bottom.

"Ceremonial bowl probably," Charlian said.

Aleshia nodded as she turned the bowl around in her hands.

"Definitely. Normal people couldn't afford this," she said.

Charlian held up the pottery shard in his hand up to the light at the top of the clearing. He couldn't make out anything special around the shard, it looked like your everyday 1000 year old shard.

"Ah," Aleshia said.

Charlian carefully put the pottery shard in his pocket and he looked at the bowl. His face lit up when he saw Aleshia was pointing to a little religious mark on the bottom. It was almost invisible to the naked eye, but after doing this for so long they both learnt what to look out for.

"Cool," Charlian said, "perfect for making sure an enemy village didn't see you worshipping false gods and kill you,"

Aleshia tutted. "Babe, I'm not a history student. I do know,"

Charlian nodded and then pointed to the high people on the edge of the clearing.

"You might not be, but they are. They might as well try to learn something in their high state,"

Aleshia playfully hit him on the head.

Charlian took the clay bowl from Aleshia and focused on the mark. Now he held it, he looked as closely as he could and it looked like the marking was of a monkey.

He had no clue if the Rouble worshipped monkeys.

"Monkeys?"

Aleshia rolled her eyes. "This… how old do you think this is?"

Charlian relooked at the bowl. The clay wasn't cracked too much, the surface was too smooth for ancient techniques and now Charlian was thinking about it. There was no historical mentions of gold findings, melting or creative uses in this region until the last two hundred years.

This wasn't a Rouble settlement.

"The thatch roofs," Charlian said, frowning.

Aleshia clicked her fingers. "I thought this wasn't thatch on second thought,"

Charlian and Aleshia went over to a massive clump of thatch that was rising out of the ground, and Charlian rubbed it with his fingers.

He knew exactly why Aleshia doubted it was thatch. They were in the middle of the rainforest, so clearly whoever lived here wouldn't have had access to the straw needed to create thatch.

And there were plenty of rainforest materials that if a clever person treated correctly, it would look but not feel like thatch.

But as Charlian kept inspecting, touching and making sure the material was thatch. He quickly realised that the material was far too thick, wooden and unbending to be a thatch roof.

It was much too likely to be manipulated bamboo, tree bark or another undiscovered plant altogether.

Aleshia started smiling and Charlian smiled too. That was a good sign for them because it meant that there was still a chance this was a Rouble settlement.

Strange animal noises echoed all around the clearing, and Charlian just looked at Aleshia. They both knew it was coming from the very high Lordic, Cassandrea and the rest of their team.

But it sounded more... pleasurable by now.

"I guess we really should get them out and back to camp for treatment," Charlian said.

He chuckled as he watched the colour, excitement and happiness drain quickly from Aleshia's face.

Charlian looked around the clearing once more, and grabbed a few different samples of the pottery, (not) thatch roof and broken wooden huts so they could test them back at the main camp.

"Come on," Charlian said, extending his hand to Aleshia.

She slowly smiled and took it. Charlian hated to think how much distress she was in, he knew she wasn't enjoying all the newfound fame as it was. Then add in Cessandrea being how she was and the nightmare of a team getting high on an expedition.

He wouldn't blame her for hating being an expedition leader. Hell, he was glad he wasn't one.

But he would support her no matter what.

"Octon!" Charlian shouted as he looked at the disgusting sight of the high team members doing creative things to each other.

Charlian had to get them back to camp and help them.

Then he had to find out who did this settlement belong to.

And that really, really thrilled him.

Finally a chance to solve a historical mystery.

CHAPTER 13

Aleshia sat on the wonderfully carved chairs at the head table inside the Mess Hut as she waited for the medical staff (fancy way of saying crew members with medical training) to get back to her.

Cassandrea was clearly stupid and so arrogant, so Aleshia was more than okay if the medical staff told her, Cassandrea needed to leave the expedition to go to a hospital in a nearby city. Aleshia really, really loved that option, but she doubted it.

Aleshia was far too good of a leader for that to happen, as soon as she saw Lordic, Cassandrea and the rest of their team were in trouble, she had made sure to get them out.

Damn her morality.

And with Octon watching over all of them, Aleshia was sure they were all going to be fine, and that stunning fiery orange dragon could and would quickly medevac them if needed.

"Okay Ales?" Charlian said, gently.

Aleshia focused on the beautiful, sexy man next to her as he bought in two large mugs of coffee.

Aleshia took her mug and she just wrapped her hands round it. On a day like this she needed the comfort.

Aleshia looked round the mess hut and thankfully it was completely empty, calm and clean of everyone and everything. The advantages of recalling everyone and giving them an early dinner.

Aleshia smiled at that. To other people she might have sounded like a mother, but she really was to these people. Aleshia loved each and every one of them like they were her own children.

"I bought the equipment," Charlian said as he lifted up a large brown backpack.

As Charlian spread out the various tubes, conical flasks and chemicals on the Head Table in front of them both, Aleshia felt her excitement build and build and build.

She loved testing the historical finds and samples to see what other secrets science could tell them.

Aleshia got out the samples of the non-thatch roof, pottery and the wooden hut that they had found in the clearing. It was a shame they weren't able to study the larger structures, but after what happened to (stupid) Cassandrea, Lordic and their team. It was just too risky.

"Right then," Charlian said. "What do you want to test first?"

Aleshia smiled and her legs started shaking in the excitement, so she got out the large clay bowl she had found with the small religious marking in the bottom.

"Let's try this. I'm guessing it's from the last two

hundred years," Aleshia said.

Charlian nodded as he stood the bowl and took a scraping of some of the clay.

Aleshia carefully picked up a test tube and added in a chemical solution and waited for Charlian to pour the scraping in. The entire idea being the colour the solution turned would tell them how old the clay was.

"Here you are babe," Charlian said.

"Thank you," Aleshia said as she swirled the test tube about.

A few seconds later the solution turned bright red and Aleshia coughed as the horrible smell of sour lemons attacked her senses. She had completely forgotten how smelly this work was sometimes.

"Red?" Charlian asked. "That's not two hundred years old,"

Aleshia rolled her eyes. He was sadly right, the chemical solution turned red because of a mineral in the solid (that was uniquely created exactly a hundred thousand years ago) that decayed over its lifetime, and when added to this particular chemical solution, the different stages of the decay turned it a different colour.

"Red means this is at least fifty thousands years old," Aleshia said slowly.

"Damn," Charlian said, "so this isn't Rouble?"

Aleshia smiled. "Not in the slightest. The mineral in the soil stops decayed after the clay sets or is baked dry, and we know fire baking clay has been around for around seventy thousand years,"

Charlian shook his head and drank his coffee. Aleshia did the same and the most amazing flavours of sharp bitter coffee, creamy milk and the burned sweetest of Maple syrup filled her mouth.

It was amazing.

"Let's try the rest of the pottery," Charlian said.

Aleshia nodded. She grabbed another test tube, added the solution and Charlian poured in some of the clay samples.

Aleshia shook the test.

Again the solution turned red.

"So all the pottery is from another settlement. At least 50,000 years old?" Aleshia asked.

She didn't know it turned into a question, but she was just hoping for something concrete about the Rouble tribe.

The tribe has definitely been a thousand years old, but they just kept finding other settlements from different eras. It was damn well annoying!

"Um?" Charlian said, gesturing for Aleshia to give him an idea.

Aleshia looked at the other samples and there was no point checking them. If they were from different historical settlements then the settlements would have been built on top of each other.

Aleshia knew all the pottery, wooden huts and non-thatch roofs would have belonged to the same tribe and not the Rouble tribe.

This was yet another dead end.

Aleshia just wanted, needed to find a single

Rouble Tribe settlement and find out what the Deer meant to the tribe.

The mess Hut shook.

Benches flipped.

Aleshia jumped up.

Charlian gently placed his hands on her.

"What is it Octon!" Charlian shouted.

Aleshia rolled her eyes. Trust that dragon to make such an unneeded commotion.

"It's Lordic Boss!" Octon shouted.

Aleshia felt her stomach tighten.

"What's wrong?" Aleshia asked.

"Girly, Boss," Octon said, "Lordic's dead,"

CHAPTER 14

Charlian couldn't believe this was happening. He had never had a death on an expedition before (well, not like this).

As Octon pointed them towards a small wooden hut, Charlian and Aleshia entered it, and Charlian instantly hated the horribly strong smell of burning sage. It was disgusting.

Then Charlian focused on the two wooden medical beds, five wooden chairs and the two angry looking women dressed in white staring at him.

It took Charlian a few more moments to notice that now two bodies were laying on the medical beds. It looked like Lordic and a female member of the team were just sleeping peacefully. But they were dead.

Dead and cold.

Charlian opened his mouth to say something, but he couldn't. He didn't know what to say in the slightest, this was impossible. It just didn't seem real.

Charlian kissed Aleshia on the head as she clung to him. Charlian had no idea how she was dealing with all this, she was Lead on the expedition so all these deaths would be her responsibility.

Charlian hated the idea of that. He was definitely going to help her.

"You!" Cassandrea shouted.

Charlian and Aleshia both looked at the wooden chairs and noticed Cassandrea and three other members of her team were weakly sitting there drinking some strange bright red concoction.

"You killed my husband!" Cassandrea shouted.

She shot up. Charlian stood in front of Aleshia. He wasn't letting Cassandrea hurt her.

Cassandrea stumbled over to Charlian. Getting right in his face.

"You bastards! My husband-"

"It is not our fault," Charlian said.

"You saw us high. You didn't get help straight away, Professors!" one of the team members said.

Charlian wasn't going to confirm that to them. If that little detail got out then… he didn't know, Aleshia and him would probably be done in the history community forever. No more sponsors, no more expeditions, no more anything.

But maybe that would be a good thing. Maybe it's what Aleshia would want, but perhaps she was too scared to admit it.

"We didn't think you were in danger," Charlian said.

Aleshia pushed away from him. "We didn't think you were in danger right away,"

Both of the two women dressed in white shook their heads. "Professors, we are the medical staff of the Expedition. It is our duty to write up a report of the facts of these two unnatural deaths,"

Charlian swore under his breath. The only reason he had forgotten about that duty was because no one had ever died suspiciously on an expedition he had been on.

But now the two medical staff had said it, Charlian was really not looking forward to the interviews, interrogations and evidence gathering. All because these two medical staff had to explain the case before a Grand Jury at the Historical Association.

This is not what Charlian needed, or Aleshia for that matter. If anything happened she was going to suffer a lot more as she was Lead.

"What do you need?" Aleshia said kindly.

"You to die!" Cassandrea shouted.

She flew at Aleshia.

Charlian jumped in front.

Cassandrea swung.

Whacking Charlian in the face.

Then the two medical staff simply walked over to Cassandrea and injected her with something. Her body went limp instantly and the medical staff placed her back on the chair.

Charlian half-smiled at Aleshia, but she wasn't

happy. Charlian wasn't going to try and convince her now it was in their best interest. Because it wasn't.

Both their reputations could and would be destroyed now if the medical staff deemed their actions to be reckless.

Where they?

Charlian wasn't sure. When he saw Cassandrea, Lordic and their team were high on drugs, he didn't think anything of it. He just assumed they would be okay sooner or later when he got them back to camp, but now… he just wasn't so sure.

The two medical staff pointed to the door and Charlian, Aleshia and the two women went outside. Charlian still loved the hot humid air, but it was clear it was really, really annoying Aleshia.

"We will write our report," the medical staff both said. "We know of the plant they got high off and it should have been detailed in your research report and risk assessment,"

Charlian really wished he had read those before he came here with Aleshia. But considering she was in charge of the expedition and getting the sponsorship approved, she could have known about the toxic plants.

As much as Charlian didn't want to think about it, he had to wonder, did Aleshia actually want Cassandrea to die?

"Do you need anything from us?" Aleshia asked.

The two women looked at each other. "Is anything Cassandrea said not true? Did you see them and not think about removing them straight away?"

Aleshia looked at Charlian with her eyes widened and wet. He wasn't going to screw this up for his beautiful wife, but he also didn't want to lie. It was dishonest and the military had bred lying out of him.

Except if you needed to protect the ones you loved. And he loved Aleshia more than anything else in the world.

"Yes. We categorically did not know about the dangerous plant that killed Lordic. We did not know that plant releasing the drugs could or would kill him," Charlian said.

And Charlian knew that was not a lie in the slightest. He didn't know the plants would do that.

The two women looked at each other and cocked their heads.

"We'll note it down but the medical situation was still clear. Hence you both broke the rules,"

Charlian watched Aleshia turn her hands into fists.

"So we will write our reports and submit it to the Historical Association in the morning. Then I suspect the Association will summon you both back tomorrow afternoon,"

Charlian fell forward. His stomach tightened into a crippling knot.

"So I suggest you two get on with the expedition. You have less than 18 hours to find your Deer," the women said as they went back into the Medical Hut.

Charlian and Aleshia just looked at each other.

This was unthinkable.

They had to find the Deer and Rouble settlements.

They couldn't fail. They had to find out the truth.

Tons of people coughed behind them.

Charlian and Aleshia turned around to see every single member of the expedition there smiling and holding maps, climbing equipment and textbooks.

They clearly didn't want Charlian and Aleshia to fail, and that made them delighted.

Aleshia just looked at Charlian. "Come on honey. We have a lost tribe to find,"

CHAPTER 15
10 Hours Left

Aleshia hated the damn Historical Association, their rules and definitely Charlian. He never should have admitted their mistake, why the hell did he do it?

Aleshia was flat out furious.

As Aleshia sat at the wonderfully carved Head table the smell of sweat was overwhelming inside the Mess Hut as every single member of the crew was reading textbooks, studying artefacts and trying to find any mention of an actual Rouble settlement.

They had to find one.

Everyone had worked constantly through the night and even after silly Charlian had ordered everyone to get two hours of sleep, everyone had come back working even harder.

There was no time to waste, and Aleshia was starting to feel the sweat drip down her back as she focused more and more on where the Rouble tribe could have set up.

As much as Aleshia hated herself and her silly husband for what happened to Lordic and the other poor soul, she had to focus. She was not going to go into that stuffy chamber at the Historical Association with all those stuck up idiots without bringing them a historical find.

Then Aleshia stopped reading the textbook she was flipping through. Maybe she had changed too much in recent weeks, she never thought of the Association as stuck up before or needing to bring them something. She studied history for the fun of it, but she couldn't help but wonder if the fun was gone now?

"Professors!" someone shouted.

Aleshia and Charlian stood up and went over to the large group of crew members who were all crowded round a single young woman flicking through an art book filled with the paintings and drawings of the Rouble tribe. Charlian had been flicking through it too.

"Yes," Aleshia said, "what have you found?"

The young woman with her awful black teeth and rags for clothes slowly got up and smiled.

"Professor, if you carefully look at each drawing and painting there is a single feature that pops up in each one," the woman said.

Aleshia went over to her and tried not to gag as the woman stunk of sweat, grease and even poo. She really, really needed a wash.

"Here Professor," the woman said pointing to

each of the four images on the page.

Aleshia focused on where the woman was pointing, and after a few moments Aleshia realised that in each image, there was a minor drawing of a flower.

It wasn't like anything Aleshia had ever seen before, it was in the shape of a Rose, but it had massive spikes, black leaves and the centre of the flower looked like the mouth of a snake.

"Anyone ever seen this before?" Aleshia said.

Everyone shook their heads, and Aleshia even heard some stupid crew members mutter if Professor Cassandrea knew better. Aleshia was really having enough of those elements of her crew.

Charlian shook his head. "It isn't a flower,"

Aleshia looked at him and there was just something about his soft warm eyes, and all the hate, rage and fury Aleshia had built up just melted away. Charlian wasn't her enemy, she really, really loved him.

"What is it then babe?"

"It's symbolic," Charlian said, "remember the Great White Deer appears in 3 areas of Rouble mythology,"

Aleshia clicked her fingers. "We talked about the Creation stories earlier. Then we know the Deer turns up in the Great Hunt and the Blood Drinking. How do they connect to this flower?"

Charlian smiled. "The black leaves represent the dying Deer that the Rouble tribe kill for their rose-coloured blood. Then the killing of the Deer breeds new life into the Tribe like the growing of a new flower,"

Aleshia smiled that was amazing. It was wonderful to know that the Rouble were so creative and bright, but it didn't help them find a Rouble settlement.

Or did it?

Aleshia carefully snatched the art book away from the smelly woman and flicked through all the drawings, looking at each individual piece of artwork.

They were all stunningly beautiful and perfect, considering the Rouble Tribe was relatively primitive. But Aleshia was much more interested in where the little Rose turned up, and then she realised that a pattern was emerging.

The Rouble Tribe were extremely clever people and they were also obsessed with the importance of mythology and being able to hide secrets away in case they were attacked and destroyed by another tribe.

Aleshia knew it was extremely common back in the day.

And the more pieces of artwork Aleshia studied the more she was starting to understand why the Rouble people loved artwork so much. It was an amazing way to hide messages.

Including the position of one of your major settlements. Aleshia knew it was a long shot, but from the conversations Aleshia had had with Lordic the rainforest wasn't as developed as it was today. Like the desert was a lot closer to the Rouble than it would have been today.

Aleshia pointed to the artwork. "Look how these twenty artwork pieces are of the desert in the South,"

Everyone nodded.

"And you see the Rose is in the far left-hand corner at the top," Aleshia said.

Everyone nodded again.

Aleshia turned a few pages. "Now these next twenty images are more in the centre of the rainforest where we believe the Rouble to be located,"

"Okay," Charlian said.

"And the Rose is a lot closer to the centre than before. I would say most of the time the image is just on the left-hand side. Not too far left, not too close to the centre,"

Aleshia flipped to the pieces of art in the centre of the art book. "Now look,"

Charlian smiled and everyone gasped.

Aleshia pointed to the little Rose that were all drawn in the dead centre of the image. Aleshia fully believed that the location of the Rose in the image and what the images were about were clues to the location of a major Rouble settlement.

It was an absolutely perfect method to hide information. The Rouble would simply give out images to their friends and themselves so they would work out how to find the settlement for themselves.

"So if this is right," Charlian said, "how do we find this settlement?"

Aleshia smiled. She had a very rough idea, so she turned to the exact middle page of the artwork, and pointed to the only image where the little Rose icon was at the dead centre of the image.

That image was a drawing of a waterfall.

Charlian's eyes widened. "Wow,"

Aleshia was expecting a little more but she understood. If this turned out to be true then she would have decrypted and solved one of the biggest mysteries surrounding the Rouble Tribe.

Then Aleshia smelt horrible hints of sweat, grease and poo as every single member of the crew congratulated her and hugged her.

They all loved and respected Aleshia, and that made her damn proud of herself, Charlian and them all.

They were a team.

But with time running out Aleshia knew they had to find the settlement quickly before their chance was lost forever.

CHAPTER 16
3 Hours Left

As Charlian stood in front of a massive churning lake the size of three football pitches that was connected to a waterfall the height of a small mountain, he had to admit he had never ever met a waterfall that was so hard to find.

It had taken them seven hours with teams exploring the rainforest on foot, climbing up trees and Charlian and Aleshia flying on Octon to be able to find this stupid waterfall that was meant to solve all their problems.

With only three hours to go until the Association summoned them, Charlian was starting to get really concerned. They just had to find out the truth about the Rouble Tribe and what the Great Deer meant to them.

As Octon with her beautiful fiery orange scales landed with the last of the crew members, Charlian watched her stomp over to a massive brown tree (that lined the entire lake) and fall down.

She was clearly resting after her (not) busy flight.

"Where do we start?" everyone asked.

Charlian just looked at Aleshia who was standing next to him, and now with the entire crew standing just metres from him. Charlian really understood the sweaty, greasy smell that Aleshia mentioned earlier. It was disgusting.

Then he realised Aleshia looked fearful, scared and even a little shocked at the question.

"Come on honey," Charlian said quietly, "you're still Expedition Lead,"

Aleshia smiled at that, kissed Charlian and ordered everyone to start searching the lake, waterfall and hopefully the top of the waterfall to check for any sign of the Rouble Tribe.

"Octon!" Charlian shouted.

Octon smiled and slowly forced herself up, and Charlian realised she wasn't faking being tired. He had to remember to give her a few days to herself, or do whatever she wanted to do with him after this expedition.

"Yeah boss," she said.

"Take some crew members up to the top please," Charlian said with a smile.

Octon muttered something and scooped up the closest five crew members and flew them to the top of the waterfall.

Then Charlian went to the edge of the lake and was surprised to see all the white foam that the waterfall was creating because of the sheer force the water was coming over at. Charlian wouldn't like to even remotely guess at what would happen if someone got caught in that water.

They would probably be crushed before they died of drowning.

And Charlian couldn't understand the strange smell coming from the water. It was almost a sulphur type of smell that was absolutely horrific. It started making Charlian feel a bit lightheaded, and the outrageous taste of rotten eggs formed on his tongue.

"God-King!" Aleshia shouted. "What is that smell?"

Charlian smiled and pointed to the water. Aleshia and Charlian both covered their mouth and noses with cloth. But even that didn't help, Charlian could still taste rotten eggs in his mouth.

"What could cause that?" Aleshia asked, sounding more interested than disgusted.

"I don't know. It makes no sense. This should be clean, pure rainforest water," Charlian said.

"Yea. If the sulfur or whatever it is was in the water, then the entire rainforest would be dead beyond this point,"

Charlian looked behind them and realised all the rainforest and massive brown trees were perfectly healthy.

"So these trees behind us," Charlian said, "can't be using this water either. Otherwise they would be dead,"

Aleshia cocked her head and nodded. "No plants are using this water. Why?"

"What do you mean?" Charlian asked.

"Come on Charlie, this lake would have to be made from really solid rock to stop any tree roots from making their way there,"

Charlian had to agree with that, it was basic biology that plant roots moved towards the closest source of water. So why didn't the roots from the surrounding trees move here?

"And why did the Rouble Tribe love this location?" Charlian asked.

They both stood up and Charlian pointed towards the rather stunning waterfall.

"I guess it's beautiful, but there's no practical choices here,"

Aleshia clicked her fingers. "Remember babe. Whenever it comes to religious sites no one is logical. We need to remember this in the context that the Roubles were obsessed with their mythology,"

"Of course. Didn't they believe in Water Goblins and Mermans?" Charlian asked.

"They did, and… where's that artbook?" Aleshia asked.

Charlian waved over the young woman with horrible teeth and Aleshia asked her for the art book. Once Aleshia had it she flicked open a page with four images of a massive waterfall and without fail every image contained drawings of Water Goblins.

"This must have been a holy site for them,"

Charlian said, "and what better place to find Deer,"

Aleshia cocked her head.

Charlian blew her a kiss. It made perfect sense to him.

"This location is home to a massive Lake. It's a perfect place for Deer to come and drink water, so considering the Deer that live in the rainforest are believed to be magical. Then the Rouble probably believed the Great White Deer would come here to talk to the other magical creatures,"

"Like the Water Goblins and Mermans," Aleshia said.

"Exactly," Charlian said.

Charlian led Aleshia back over to the Lake and he carefully looked over the edge into the foamy churning water.

"If the Rouble believed Deer would come here, then they would have wanted to create a structure to help them with their Great Deer Hunts and the blood drinking," Charlian said.

Aleshia nodded. "What you thinking? A shack or something for them to store the meat, drain the blood and whatever they use the Deer corpses for?"

Charlian cocked his head. He wasn't exactly sure it would be a shack, but considering how important the Great White Deer was to the Rouble Tribe. He could only imagine they would create something rather grand to honour their most holy creature or being.

Then for a split second the white foamy water

stopped and went perfectly still. Just long enough for Charlian to see something big, black and maybe wooden in the water.

And now it all made sense to Charlian, if there was something under the water, then that just might be the amazing find that they needed to bring back to the Historical Association.

But there was no hope of seeing anything unless the water was stopped.

"Octon!" Charlian shouted as loud as he could.

+What ya want my fav boss?+ Octon sent into his mind.

Charlian had completely forgotten Octon could mind talk with him.

+I need you to block the water+ Charlian sent.

+Come on boss. Ya know I love ya but I ain't going stop no water. That hard+

+Please my beautiful Octon. I need you. Can you knock down some trees and block the waterfall that way+

Charlian fell to his knees as Octon's laughter filled his mind.

+Na boss. I gonna do ya one better+

Charlian let out a deep breath as he felt Octon disconnect their mental link and a few seconds later the waterfall stopped.

+Hurry up Boss! There's so much water pounding me!+

Charlian almost felt numb as he realised Octon was laying down at the top of the waterfall. He couldn't even begin to imagine the sheer force of that water pounding into her.

Charlian just looked at Aleshia. "We need to hurry,"

As soon as the words had left his mouth, Charlian gasped as the lake stopped churning and all the crew members wandered over to see something beautiful.

There was a building under the water.

Charlian couldn't make it out yet.

But it was a sign of hope.

CHAPTER 17
2 Hours Left

Aleshia flat out couldn't believe what she was seeing. She would have imagined it was just impossible for something to live below the water in the deep lake. But the truth was right in front of her.

As Aleshia, Charlian and the entire expedition crew focused on the black wooden structure at the bottom of the lake, Aleshia tried to imagine what it was. She had no idea.

But at least the horrific smell of sulfur stopped as the foaming water slowed, become still and the foam simply disappeared. Aleshia didn't know what Octon had done, but she was extremely grateful.

Yet just in case Octon was in pain (Aleshia had no idea why she would be), Aleshia really, really wanted to hurry up and find out what was at the bottom of the lake and why was it important to the Rouble.

That was if it was important at all.

As Aleshia felt her stomach tighten, she realised she really shouldn't be thinking like that now. For the next two hours, she had to focus completely on completing the goal of the expedition.

And that was to simply find out what the Great White Deer truly meant to the Rouble Tribe.

"What is it?" everyone started whispering to themselves.

Aleshia wanted to offer up some amazing historical answers, but she was stuck, and thankfully she didn't hear any stupid answers like *I wonder if Professor Cassandrea knows better*.

It was only then that Aleshia realised how grateful she was that Cassandrea had left with the two medical staff for the Headquarters of the Historical Association to submit their report. Aleshia had no doubt whatsoever that Cassandrea going and explaining the emotional trauma of the deaths would only damn her further.

But she didn't care. Aleshia had a job to do.

Charlian turned away from the lake and focused on everyone. Aleshia smiled at him, he was thinking something, and Aleshia loved that.

"We know the Rouble loved their mythology. They would have built something grand here to honour their mythical beings," Charlian said.

"Yo Professors, can't we just swim down to look at it?" a young man asked at the very back of the crew.

Aleshia forced herself not to smile. The lake was

easily ten, twenty metres deep and unless any of the crew were experienced divers with training on holding their breath for at least ten minutes at any one time. It was impossible for them to swim down, study the area and maybe get a few samples.

Aleshia had used diving equipment on past expeditions, but diving equipment was the last thing she ever considered bringing to the rainforest.

Sure Aleshia had done plenty of swimming as a child and teenager, she had even held her breath underwater for five minutes, but even she doubted she could do what was needed without the equipment.

Aleshia jumped when Charlian tapped her shoulder. And she realised everyone was staring at her.

"Sorry what was that?" Aleshia said.

Charlian kissed her on the head. "I was saying that because of the sulfur smell the water is probably extremely dangerous,"

"Definitely," Aleshia said.

But there just had to be a way to find out what was down there. Aleshia wondered if it was a good idea to go back to the main camp and get some massive glass containers to look through when they were in the water. Yet that wouldn't work.

Unless Octon could be useful again.

Aleshia looked at Charlian. "What if Octon goes down?"

Charlian cocked his head. "What!"

"Hear me out. Dragons have extremely strong scales. They survive the strongest acid and chemical attacks, and they don't feel pain if the scales are attacked,"

Charlian waved his hands about. "But their eyes aren't?"

"Please Charlian," Aleshia said, "can you please ask her through that weird mind talking thingy?"

Charlian looked as if he was about to argue but he smiled and nodded and closed his eyes.

After a few seconds, Charlian looked at Aleshia in shock.

"She can do it without her eyes being injured. But we have another problem," Charlian said.

"What?" Aleshia asked.

For some reason (Aleshia had no idea why), the entire expedition crew moved closer to Charlian to hear the problem.

"She's the only thing stopping the waterfall. If she moves then… the lake will start churning again,"

Aleshia frowned. "Meaning there's a risk Octon could get swept up in the force of the churning water and drown,"

Charlian slowly nodded.

As much as Aleshia hated that idea. She loved Octon almost like a best friend, but Aleshia needed to find out what was happening.

Unless they were overcomplicating it.

Aleshia simply turned towards the lake and focused on it. It was risky to do anything in the water containing the foul sulfur smell, but she just had to find out what was going on with the Rouble, The Great White Deer and its importance.

Aleshia ran towards the lake.

Charlian tried to grab her.

Aleshia jumped.

Splashing into the lake.

Her head went under.

CHAPTER 18
1.75 Hours Left

Charlian flat out hated Aleshia's rashness.

Charlian rushed over to the edge of the lake. He couldn't see his wife. He had to find her. He couldn't let her die.

Then after a few seconds that felt like years to Charlian, Aleshia's head popped back up above the water. She was thankfully alive and as much as Charlian wanted to blow her a kiss to show her how happy he was.

He just couldn't believe she had risked her own life so pointlessly. Especially since they had only said to the crew members the dangers of the water.

But the more Charlian stared at his beautiful, sexy wife, the more he realised that she was fine and she was probably the only crew member who could swim back to the large black wooden structure under the water, with her swimming experience as a teenager.

With the disgusting smell of sulfur and taste of rotten eggs completely gone, Charlian knew that whatever dangers that had been here were gone, and thankfully that meant sexy Aleshia would be okay.

"You really think you can dive down there?" Charlian asked.

He heard everyone behind him take a few steps closer.

"Yeah," Aleshia said as she took a massive breath and dived down.

Charlian and everyone else went to the very edge of the lake at the bottom of the (now empty) waterfall) and they all watched Aleshia swim down to the bottom.

Charlian knew he never ever could have done such a thing. The lake was at least ten to twenty metres deep and Aleshia would need to have a little look around, so he just hoped (or prayed or panicked) that she would be okay.

Charlian watched her little dark shape slice through the water and disappear. Charlian felt his stomach churn, twist and tighten as he feared she had gone into a building and she would get trapped there.

He didn't want her to drown and all this worrying was useless, so Charlian decided he had to act somehow.

Charlian turned to face everyone. "What could that structure be?"

Everyone shrugged.

Charlian just shook his head. These crew

members were meant to be some of the brightest students the Realm had to offer, so surely they could guess about a little wooden structure underwater?

A shrine? A tomb? A Temple?

To most non-historians they might have all been the same thing, but to Charlian they were extremely different. But Aleshia was still down there.

It had to be at least a minute or two or three, Charlian just wanted her to be okay.

Then something splashed and Charlian and everyone looked over to the far side of the lake, and saw Aleshia climbing out of the lake.

Charlian rushed over.

He picked up Aleshia in his arms and instantly put her down. There must have been something strange or dead in the water as Aleshia's skin was covered in a very thin layer of slim.

"So?" Charlian asked.

Aleshia frowned and looked to the ground. "It has to be a shrine of some kind. But… but there are so many bodies. Human, Deer and Monkey alike,"

Charlian hugged Aleshia and forced himself to tolerate the horrible feeling of slim on her skin. But what she said was beyond strange, and judging by the mutterings of the crew, they agreed.

"The Deer corpses we can attribute to the Rouble's Great Deer Hunt," Charlian said. "Did they have any markings?"

Aleshia nodded. "Yeah. Each one had the markings of being bled and their organs harvested,"

"For tha suppers!" someone said from the back.

Charlian gave them a thumb-up. "So they clearly use to hunt the Deer at this lake, move the corpses into that wooden building and prepare them for their rituals,"

Aleshia waved her finger. "No. It isn't wooden. Only the roof is, the entire building is made from boulders,"

Charlian smiled. "Boulders like in their creation story,"

There was a massive wave of groans as everyone started to understand what the Great White Deer meant to the Rouble Tribe.

Aleshia and Charlian clicked their fingers at the same time.

"I know what happened," they both said.

Charlian just loved it when that happened. It was amazing how even after so long, they were thinking the same and surprising each other.

"We've been thinking about Deer all wrong," Aleshia said.

Charlian nodded. "Exactly. We've been thinking the Great White Deer was just another part of their mythology. But it isn't. It's the King of their Mythology,"

All the crew members sounded confused.

"Think about it this way," Aleshia said to them, "in their creation story the Great White Deer created the world out of a boulder with its death creating rainforests and other features of the world,"

Everyone nodded.

"And," Charlian said, "just look at their artwork, paintings and drawings. The Rouble Tribe loved the world,"

A few crew members shrugged.

"What my husband means," Aleshia said, "is the Rouble didn't care about Gods, Goddesses and mythical creatures. They cared about the physical world, and if they believed the Great White Deer created, and gave them their beautiful world to paint and create art from,"

"Then the Deer was the most precious thing in all of creation to them," Charlian said.

As Charlian watched everyone smile, he just stood there nodding. Because he understood exactly why they all looked so happy and pleased, because there was such beauty in the story of the Great White Deer.

There were so many stories in history that taught the modern world to focus on war, Kings and each other. But Charlian always felt like something was missing, and now he had found it.

He had finally found a story or area of history that taught him to focus on the real natural beauty that was all around him, Aleshia and their amazing crew.

He would definitely take that away with him.

The waterfall roared.

Millions of litres gushed over the edge.

Slamming into the lake.

Making it turn violent.

Charlian pulled Aleshia back.

Octon flew overhead. She was scared. She was panicked.

"They're here!" Octon shouted.

Charlian was just about to ask what when he saw five massive dragons with blood red scales land on top of the waterfall, and then another five dragons landed all around Charlian, Aleshia and the crew.

They were trapped.

A deafening shriek pierced the air and made Charlian look up at the top of the waterfall where a woman in solid gold armour stood staring at him and Aleshia.

"Professor Aleshia and Charlian O'Kin," the woman said, her voice booming. "You are coming with us. You have been found guilty of manslaughter, dereliction of duty and the Defraudment of the Historical Association,"

Charlian grabbed onto Aleshia. If anything happened he had to protect her.

But Aleshia simply turned around and smiled. "You know they wouldn't hurt us. They just want us gone from the Association,"

"You are coming by choice," the woman said, "or force?"

Charlian looked at Aleshia and nodded. He trusted, loved and respected her more than anyone else in the entire world.

"We go by choice," Aleshia said.

As Charlian listened to the crew members moan, groan and resist as the other Dragon Riders pushed through them, he just gripped Aleshia's hand tight and he focused on the amazing black structure below them.

So much history left to explore.

But no more time.

They had come early.

But Charlian had discovered what the Great White Deer meant.

And that thrilled him.

But the future terrified him.

CHAPTER 19

As Charlian sat in the little stone prison cell after the Historical Association Court hearing, he felt so happy with himself and Aleshia. Finally they were going to be free once more, with some major changes along the way.

In a few moments (he hoped) Charlian really looked forward to getting out of here, kissing his wife and leaving this entire strange episode behind.

At least that way he could get away from the horrible smell of stale urine in the cell. That made the taste of cheap, awful beer form on his tongue. It was foul!

But he'd be lying if he said he wasn't unnerved by it all.

It was even stranger that only a few days ago Charlian's worry had been focused on the expedition and all the dangerous predators that lived there. Charlian had been scared of the creatures in the main camp and hurting Aleshia, that had been his fear.

But Charlian had clearly forgotten one of the most important rules from his military days, and he just felt silly for it now. He had forgotten that most of the time, the enemy and predators and killers weren't the people he would believe them to be.

Just like believing that the rainforest was the biggest threat to him, Aleshia and the expedition, it turned out that Charlian's own people had been the dangerous predators. And they pounced and killed him and his sexy wife.

Considering he had never been inside a Historical Association hearing before, Charlian was rather impressed with it all. There had been so many academics and other stuck-up people on chairs in a circle with Charlian and Aleshia in the centre.

They all quickly casted their judgement.

But Charlian still had to laugh at the stupidity of some of those charges. Some of them (like them like the fraud charge) must have been dreamed up by some high drugged-up academic (there were plenty of them about, and not just in the rainforest!) because Charlian and Aleshia never used Association money on their expeditions because they were independent of any university.

Yet that manslaughter charge was still paining him. Charlian never wanted Lordic to die, he was a good man, a man that just wanted to help them and a man that loved what he did. Charlian flat out loved all of those features of Lordic.

Now no one would ever know or get to meet

him, and learn from that amazing mind.

All because of him.

Of course Charlian knew it wasn't really his fault, him and Aleshia had been wanting to explore history, teach annoying people a lesson and make Cassandrea less arrogant. It clearly hadn't worked, and now a good man had paid the price.

So when the stuck-up academics had given their judgement to Charlian and Aleshia of guilty. He understood it. He understood why they were kicking them out of the Association and in all honesty, Charlian was glad.

Sure they could never be apart of any expedition again, or organise their own or do anything to do with history. But maybe that was a good thing.

Charlian knew that Aleshia had fallen out of love with the business-side of history for a few weeks. And it was only now that Charlian had been forced out, that he understood that he had lost his love too.

Ever since they got famous, there were so many people coming to them, banging on about them and hounding them to do talks, write books and do more academic research into history.

But history was never ever about any of that for Charlian. It certainly wasn't for Aleshia too.

Charlian had left the military (for Aleshia mainly) because he wanted to explore, study and discover ground-breaking history. Which he had done multiple times, even on this last expedition which Charlian had no doubt would be recorded in history as "The Fatal

Expedition of The Rouble" him, Aleshia and their wonderful crew had rewritten what was known about the Rouble.

So, so few people ever got the chance to say that.

But clearly the politics of the Association just didn't want them anymore.

And that was that.

Charlian might not have known what he was going to do next with his life, but he loved Aleshia and that was all he had ever needed.

And that certainly wasn't going to change anytime soon.

CHAPTER 20

It might have only been a few days since Aleshia was last at the museum but it felt like nothing, and everything changed in that short time.

Only a few days ago she had come here as a historian, a person who loved researching the past and informing others about it. And now she actually didn't know what she was returning as.

The part of the museum Aleshia was standing in was a long black corridor with the amazing smell of sweet lemons and other chemical smells that were perfect here. To Aleshia, it meant the museum was clean, safe and the artefacts were protected. And the added bonus of the taste of lemon cheesecake forming on her tongue.

Considering everything that had happened in the past few days, from the deaths to the amazing discovery to the hearing, Aleshia just didn't know what had happened.

Her life had been so fixed, so predictable and

wonderful that it made no sense where it had gone wrong. But deep down Aleshia knew exactly what had happened.

She had gotten famous, and success always annoyed people. But that never stopped her, if people got annoyed at her, it was because she had done amazing and that's what she wanted everyone to be and do.

But sometimes success creates powerful enemies, especially in such a clicky, political organisation like the Historical Association, so Cassandrea had become an enemy. And sought to destroy Aleshia and her handsome husband, and so she did.

Aleshia knew history would fall, the research would stop and even the general public would start to pay less interest in it over time. But that wasn't her problem, because Aleshia had finally realised what was important in her life.

Aleshia might have started being a historian because of her parents and how famous they were with their legendary discoveries. But that was never ever what she had truly wanted to do, Aleshia had stayed in history because she liked the work, and it was amazing trying to solve the mysteries of the past.

Yet what Aleshia had always wanted to do, was just to be loved by a handsome man and make her own choices.

Before she set off for the expedition, she had fully believed that her feelings of sadness was about not knowing if she wanted to work in history anymore. And she was only half-right.

In reality (and it was clear as day now to Aleshia), she was only concerned and tired of all the fame, attention and everything else. Because they all made her realise history was not what she wanted to do anymore.

Of course, Aleshia was confused as anything about what to do next. She had lived, breathed and been involved in history literally ever since she was born, with all the travelling her family did for their parents' expeditions.

So in a way this newfound freedom was so alien to Aleshia.

The amazing smell of lemons was subtly replaced with the stunning smell of fried fish and chips that were so fresh, Aleshia could still smell the salt in the air.

Aleshia smiled to her handsome husband that was so damn cute as he walked over to her with Octon carefully walking him. As Charlian held a fresh bag of fish and chips.

Aleshia really looked forward to that, and it just showed her everything she ever needed.

Herself, Charlian and Octon were family. A great loving family that Aleshia never wanted to lose, and both her and Charlian were young and she did want kids, so their family would only grow. And that was amazing.

It wasn't even like they needed the money, or the work. Aleshia and Charlian had been to so many speaking engagements, written so many articles and taught so much at the university (three classes was a lot for them) that they had had too much money.

They had saved more than enough to keep them going for the rest of their lives.

Aleshia looked at the little half-deer, half-man statue that she had looked at only days ago, and she felt nothing for it. Back the Historical Association had forced her, Aleshia was done with history. She would buy a book or two from time to time, but nothing of the past.

Aleshia only wanted to focus on the future.

So Aleshia went over to Charlian, wrapped an arm around his waist and kissed him. Aleshia smiled as she tasted the salty fish on his lips, she loved him so damn much.

Then Aleshia went to say something, but both Charlian and Octon just smiled at her, and Aleshia realised there was nothing she needed to say. They were all an amazing family that loved each other no matter what.

And as Aleshia, Charlian and Octon walked out of the Museum, she wanted to ask about the past and how they were dealing with everything.

But when they had all lived in the past for so long, she knew it was going to be great living in the present and future for a while.

And Aleshia would never disagree.

GET YOUR FREE AND EXCLUSIVE SHORT STORY NOW! LEARN ABOUT NEMESIO'S PAST!

https://www.subscribepage.com/fircheart

Keep up to date with exclusive deals on Connor Whiteley's Books, as well as the latest news about new releases and so much more!

Sign up for the Grab a Book and Chill Monthly newsletter, and you'll get one **FREE** ebook just for signing up: Agents of The Emperor Collection.

Sign Up Now!

https://dl.bookfunnel.com/f4p5xkprbk

About the author:

Connor Whiteley is the author of over 60 books in the sci-fi fantasy, nonfiction psychology and books for writer's genre and he is a Human Branding Speaker and Consultant.

He is a passionate warhammer 40,000 reader, psychology student and author.

Who narrates his own audiobooks and he hosts The Psychology World Podcast.

All whilst studying Psychology at the University of Kent, England.

Also, he was a former Explorer Scout where he gave a speech to the Maltese President in August 2018 and he attended Prince Charles' 70th Birthday Party at Buckingham Palace in May 2018.

Plus, he is a self-confessed coffee lover!

OTHER SHORT STORIES BY CONNOR WHITELEY

Blade of The Emperor
Arbiter's Truth
The Bloodied Rose
Asmodia's Wrath
Heart of A Killer
Emissary of Blood
Computation of Battle
Old One's Wrath
Puppets and Masters
Ship of Plague
Interrogation
Edge of Failure
One Way Choice
Acceptable Losses
Balance of Power
Good Idea At The Time
Escape Plan
Escape In The Hesitation
Inspiration In Need
Singing Warriors
Dragon Coins
Dragon Tea
Dragon Rider
Knowledge is Power
Killer of Polluters

THE GREAT DEER

Climate of Death
Sacrifice of the Soul
Heart of The Flesheater
Heart of The Regent
Heart of The Standing
Feline of The Lost
Heart of The Story
The Family Mailing Affair
Defining Criminality
The Martian Affair
A Cheating Affair
The Little Café Affair
Mountain of Death
Prisoner's Fight
Claws of Death
Bitter Air
Honey Hunt
Blade On A Train
City of Fire
Awaiting Death
Poison In The Candy Cane
Christmas Innocence
You Better Watch Out
Christmas Theft
Trouble In Christmas
Smell of The Lake
Problem In A Car

Theft, Past and Team
Embezzler In The Room
A Strange Way To Go
A Horrible Way To Go
Ann Awful Way To Go
An Old Way To Go
A Fishy Way To Go
A Pointy Way To Go
A High Way To Go
A Fiery Way To Go
A Glassy Way To Go
A Chocolatey Way To Go
Kendra Detective Mystery Collection Volume 1
Kendra Detective Mystery Collection Volume 2
Stealing A Chance At Freedom
Glassblowing and Death
Theft of Independence
Cookie Thief
Marble Thief
Book Thief
Art Thief

Other books by Connor Whiteley:

The Fireheart Fantasy Series
Heart of Fire
Heart of Lies
Heart of Prophecy
Heart of Bones
Heart of Fate

City of Assassins (Urban Fantasy)
City of Death
City of Marytrs
City of Pleasure
City of Power

Agents of The Emperor
Return of The Ancient Ones
Vigilance
Angels of Fire

The Garro Series- Fantasy/Sci-fi
GARRO: GALAXY'S END
GARRO: RISE OF THE ORDER
GARRO: END TIMES
GARRO: SHORT STORIES
GARRO: COLLECTION
GARRO: HERESY

GARRO: FAITHLESS
GARRO: DESTROYER OF WORLDS
GARRO: COLLECTIONS BOOK 4-6
GARRO: MISTRESS OF BLOOD
GARRO: BEACON OF HOPE
GARRO: END OF DAYS

Winter Series- Fantasy Trilogy Books
WINTER'S COMING
WINTER'S HUNT
WINTER'S REVENGE
WINTER'S DISSENSION

Bettie English Private Eye Series
A Very Private Woman
The Russian Case
A Very Urgent Matter
A Case Most Personal
Trains, Scots and Private Eyes
The Federation Protects

Miscellaneous:
RETURN
FREEDOM
SALVATION
Reflection of Mount Flame
The Masked One

The Great Deer

All books in 'An Introductory Series':
BIOLOGICAL PSYCHOLOGY 3RD EDITION
COGNITIVE PSYCHOLOGY THIRD EDITION
SOCIAL PSYCHOLOGY- 3RD EDITION
ABNORMAL PSYCHOLOGY 3RD EDITION
PSYCHOLOGY OF RELATIONSHIPS- 3RD EDITION
DEVELOPMENTAL PSYCHOLOGY 3RD EDITION
HEALTH PSYCHOLOGY
RESEARCH IN PSYCHOLOGY
A GUIDE TO MENTAL HEALTH AND TREATMENT AROUND THE WORLD- A GLOBAL LOOK AT DEPRESSION
FORENSIC PSYCHOLOGY
THE FORENSIC PSYCHOLOGY OF THEFT, BURGLARY AND OTHER CRIMES AGAINST PROPERTY
CRIMINAL PROFILING: A FORENSIC PSYCHOLOGY GUIDE TO FBI PROFILING AND GEOGRAPHICAL AND STATISTICAL PROFILING.

CLINICAL PSYCHOLOGY
FORMULATION IN PSYCHOTHERAPY
PERSONALITY PSYCHOLOGY AND
INDIVIDUAL DIFFERENCES
CLINICAL PSYCHOLOGY
REFLECTIONS VOLUME 1
CLINICAL PSYCHOLOGY
REFLECTIONS VOLUME 2
CULT PSYCHOLOGY
Police Psychology

www.ingramcontent.com/pod-product-compliance
Lightning Source LLC
LaVergne TN
LVHW011840060526
838200LV00054B/4121